"Ivy, there is nothing you can do about it anymore. You might think that what you did was bad, but you protected yourself and it also happened to be in the natural way, for a vampire, that is. Which you are now, so you must learn to understand, and live with the knowledge that this will be a part of your future. You will get angry, you will get thirsty, and that thirst will be to kill whoever stands in your way. In this case, the mutts were advancing on you, and you did the natural thing and retaliated with fangs."

I give her another light squeeze, which then turns into my thumb, rubbing circles on her shoulder, just as I have done in the past. I feel her loosen up a little and all the anxiety and distress fleeing her body.

Prophecy of a Vampire

by

Tania Gold

Prophecy of a Vampire

Cover Art by *Diana Carlile*

The Wild Rose Press, Inc.
PO Box 708
Adams Basin, NY 14410-0708
Visit us at www.thewildrosepress.com

Publishing History
First Edition, 2023
Trade Paperback ISBN 978-1-5092-4824-7
Digital ISBN 978-1-5092-4825-4

Published in the United States of America

Dedication

I dedicate this book to my late Grandpa and late Grandma. They were wonderful people and dedicated family figures that I wish could see the books I've written. I know they would be proud of me, and this book.

I also dedicate this book to Paul, my amazing husband. A big thank you for all those nights we stayed up reading, planning, and editing scenes whilst the kids finally went to bed. This book would have taken much longer if I didn't have the support from him.

Chapter One

ZACHARY

Los Angeles, 1924

"Zachary! Where is my water? How many times do you need to be asked?"

"Mother, I set it beside you when you asked me the first time," I say, gesturing toward the glass of water.

With a quick roll of her bleary eyes, one hand reaches over for the glass but misses, making it shatter against the floor. A high-pitched scream follows as her withering hands clutch her chest, followed by a coughing fit. Drops of red spittle rest on her chin, making me wonder whether she realizes it's blood. When she eventually recovers, a low grumble from deep within her throat emanates. I notice her knuckles turn white as she fists the sweaty bed sheet. It torments me to watch her in pain, suffering from this horrid plague.

It isn't an unfamiliar sight, though. It's been transpiring for two days now. Father seems to have caught it too, but I fear it is much worse for him. The fevers are erratic and, unfortunately, he developed into a much weaker state than Mother.

After the spasming ceases, I come to her, kneeling by the bed in hopes to console her as I did with Father.

"Are you certain you don't want the doctor to

examine you?" I ask, worry etched in my tone.

She shakes her head. "No need. It won't help."

"Why ever not? You are sick. Father too…"

With a crazed expression, she quips at me. "Because the doctor is dead. His entire family has died. Just like the rest of us will. Except you."

I shake my head, not understanding where she is going with this.

She rolls her eyes, then sits up a little straighter, pursing her lips. Although, it's clear she is suppressing the need to divulge.

Rubbing the back of my neck, I sigh, tired of the mind games. "Okay, please tell me. What is on your mind?"

"The prophecy, of course," she says with exasperation. Almost a wonder how I don't follow her thoughts.

I take a deep breath, then exhale. This needs to stop. She is becoming delirious with tales of a prophecy. "You have mentioned it before when you were in bouts of unconsciousness. But it's time to forget nonsensical stories. Focus on doing the finest we can for you, and Father to…"

But mother shakes her head, halting me. "No! You should listen to me now, Zachary. The prophecy is true. It is not a silly story."

"Okay. Explain to me again. Why it is so important to discuss this when you need to be resting instead," I say coolly, despite becoming frustrated with her.

I watch her try to put her thoughts together. My gaze follows the trickle of sweat from her forehead. No doubt the fever has gotten worse. In fact, I have had a challenging time swaying it despite the opioids she takes. I wring the cloth before wiping off the sweat, which now emanates an unpleasant odor. However, I don't get far. She suddenly grips my wrist in a lock, staring me down.

Mother purses her lips again, glaring at me as she says, "The prophecy is a vision where a vampire will become King. Then, another one to be his Queen. This tale claims that these two vampires would be born from human parents."

The air is cold and stiff as she speaks, leaving an ominous shudder to run through me. Then I remember the state my mother is currently in.

No. Vampires are not real. This is delirium. It must be.

"Mother, can we stop please? Let's simply focus on getting be—" I say but again interrupted by her.

Mother smacks her hand against the mattress. "No! Listen to me. Is today your twenty-first birthday?"

I am finding this whole topic absurd, particularly not appreciating her jibe. Still, I respond to the question.

Craning my neck slightly, now wondering why a birthday is in relation to the story, I respond to her irrelevant yet intriguing question. "Yes, it's today..."

"Well, that just coincides with the age the young man becomes a vampire."

The tops of my eyebrows furrow at her explanation. "Mother, are you insinuating something here? I'm not interested in discussing vampires. All I want is for you and Father to get better."

"Then you are just as naïve as I believe you to be. You are a part of this prophecy. I know no more about it, just that it is your future." She gives me a stare that suggests, 'argue with me and you will regret it,' then proceeds, much to my dismay. "I thought it was a dream... a woman's voice echoed throughout my sleep. She spoke of my son's future as a strong vampire. Part of an ancient prophecy. It was the oddest dream, which I thought was just that. Nothing more. Until I found out that my body no longer belonged to me but to the unexpected babe growing inside."

I stay silent, looking at the woman who delivered me into this world. She shuffles around on the wet mattress, drenched from her sweat, which no doubt must feel unpleasant. The maid resigned once she found out about the disease that developed in her district. It began spreading around the city, killing off civilians, so she left wanting to spend what could be her last days with her family. After that, I took up the role of cleaner, housekeeper, and even cooked for my family. It looks like the disease she feared had already spread to us. Soon, I expect it to reach me.

Returning to dab her forehead with the wet cloth, I respond to her sudden announcement of my future. "Mother,"—My tone remains calm—"what do you mean by 'turning into a vampire'? We all know they are not real. Perhaps you just had a peculiar nightmare." Her mouth opens, making my immediate reaction to assume she would admonish me, but before anything leaves her mouth, I deflect the topic. "Hush now, your fever is rising. Let me rinse out the cloth and reapply it to your head once more. Then I shall observe Father afterward."

As I turn, I sense a tug at the end of my shirt. I halt, shocked at her strength during this ill state. Her tone is full of bitterness that surprises and disheartens me altogether.

Her head hangs low as she laughs before glaring at me. "You are an abomination! Your Father is unknowing of it. For years, I had to live with this knowledge. Aware that there will not be a chance of a regular life with children. Now, here I lay, dying. What a waste of time!"

Caught between disappointment and astonishment at hearing the venom spewing out of her, I back away, surprised at her sudden change in mood. At first, she was quiet, then irritable, calm, and then outraged. The mood swings were becoming tiresome.

My reaction to her disheartening comments seems to trigger further resentment as she gives me an incredulous stare, then snickers. Mother simply shakes her head. "Your naivete becomes you, Zachary. Understand the words I say," she enunciates. "Your time is up. All will change after today. You will become a creature of the night. The walking dead." There is a sudden pause as a violent coughing spell passes over, leaving her hissing at the pain. Once it subsides, she looks up at me with disgust in her eyes, continuing with a weaker voice. "Boy, I'm dying and so is your father. Hell, most of our town might die too. But you? You shall live on, drinking the blood of innocent people. I'm glad I won't be around to see it unfold."

Like a stick in the mud, I stand there, trying to comprehend her words. My focus is on her as she mumbles ludicrous things to herself.

This insanity needs to end, so I put on my rare, stern tone.

"Hush now, Mother. The sickness is making you very irrational and cruel. I'm your son making it my duty and honor to care for you and Father. Even if this illness kills me too, at least I die doing the right thing by caring for the people that gave me life." I let out a deep sigh, wondering if anything is filtering through her head, then turn my head toward the separate bed where my father lays with his head on the pillow, arms crossed on his chest. His breathing has become irregular now, mouth ajar, sucking in each breath as if it was his last, the skin sagging more each day. The fever has now developed to the stage where he is in and out of consciousness. Worry builds inside of me, but I need to at least appear positive for the sake of my mother. The sense of dread in the atmosphere was increasing as hours went on, not just in our house. It was all around our town.

A bellow rings through the room as Mother screams, stilling me. I turn to look at her as she yells.

"You don't believe me? Oh, you will become one. You shall die and then turn into one of the walking dead. A vampire who will live forever, alone. Forever an evil monster."

Helpless, I try to calm her nerves, but before I could even get close, she shifts herself away from me. "Get out. Get away from me! Leave me be. I'd rather die than be with you! Oh, why me? Why was I given the duty to birth a monster?" She wails, groaning to herself, sounding full of despair.

I can't help but stare, shocked beyond belief that I can't form words. There lies my mother, dying despite my best efforts to heal her. She spits out wicked venom, declaring me an abomination in her eyes. Not wanting my aid or presence pains me. Each malicious word my mother utters goes through me like a knife twisting its way through my heart. Frustration crawls through me, making me rub the back of my neck as I walk away, moving to my father's bed instead, hoping he would be less frenzied and more loving. Only to see another victim of what the journalists termed, 'The 1924 Los Angeles pneumonic plague'.

I rub my eyes, then temples, the stress rolling off in waves, not to mention the heavy sense of sadness that surrounds me. Now, with my mother delusional, my father dead, I have only myself left.

I straighten my lower back, turning toward her, shaking my head in defeat. "If that is how you see me, then goodbye, Mother. I only wish I had been good enough for you. Farewell." I receive no response from her except for mumblings that sound like she is in pain. Finding my duffel bag, I fill it up with only a few useful belongings. Luckily, I remember the number sequence to the family safe that is kept hidden. Seconds later, there is a click and in a rush to get moving, my hands reach inside, finding a stack of money. Stuffing it all into my pocket of my best, respectable jacket, I take my last glance around the house that had been a home for the past twenty-one years.

My heart's torn in half, not knowing what to do about the situation of leaving them behind. They won't even have a funeral, which is a true shame. Solemnly, I walk out of the house and ponder if it's my turn to catch the virus like everyone else in the town. The thought of contacting the local parish crosses my mind, although it is doubtful they will do anything about my parents. The people in this town, and even the surrounding areas, are dropping like flies.

Confusion fills me, making me fearful of my bleak future. I feel alone in this world, and by the looks of things, I really am.

Chapter Two

ZACHARY

The night has since fallen after leaving my home in South Los Angeles and walking over to the next town. Although, I don't know where exactly where my destination is. Disheartened after leaving my parents behind, a plan had not been weaved yet except to get shelter. With every step, the ache in my chest grows deeper, knowing that my life had been a lie. The woman who bore me had also despised me.

Now, what I need is to find a place to rest before nightfall. I avoid strangers hoping to avoid becoming infected with this plague. While walking through the dimly lit street, the sound of jazz lures me over.

I follow the music, which leads me to what seems to be a shop of some sort. The light glows from inside and as I make my way closer, jovial laughter rings out, which seems odd considering the state the city is in. Creeping up closer to the window to see inside, my body stills at the scene before me. Shock and disgust fill me. What I find is a very forthcoming scene of half-nude women moving provocatively, rubbing themselves against men. Women sitting on men's laps, playfully wearing their hats, and cackling at what can only be assumed as the sound of sweet nothings. I don't care for these sorts of activities, full well knowing that many men give them demeaning slang. 'Babes with long gams who seem like gentle flappers during the day but enjoy the lewd acts with cake-eaters at night.' My father used to say it in the past, being opposed to this sort of behavior. I am akin to his views, finding it inappropriate, especially for a time like this. With so many people dying, instead of staying clear of other civilians, these people act in downright folly.

The night sky darkens as I continue my search for a roof over my head. A sudden ache comes firing through my gums. As the seconds go by, the ache turns into a sharp pain I can't disregard. My body weakens and I drop to my knees. Thankfully, my hands land in front first, which saves me from falling on my face. A violent scream erupts from me, and a metallic taste forms inside my mouth.

Disgusted by the tang, I spit onto the floor and, to my horror; I see deep red blood. Opening my mouth, my pointer finger touches my aching gum. It's sharp as a razor.

What in the heathens is happening to me?

"Sir, are you all right?" asks a man as he walks in the brothel's direction. He frowns, concern visible in his eyes, which I appreciate in my tormented state. Not wanting him to know the odd pain coursing through my body, I nod, forcing myself to rise and push through the pain. My mouth remains closed, hiding the red dribble seeping from my lips. I have never been a queasy person when it regarded blood, but this was beyond what I could fathom.

However, I make it my priority not to be witnessed behaving in such a way. I need to manage this freak sensation on my own.

As I stumble my way around the back alley of the building, and notice an oak door with a broken latch. I grab hold of the solid brass knob, then turn it, entering inside without being seen or overheard. Making my way through the small lobby, I glance in every direction to check if there is anyone around. As the moments go by and I hear nothing, nor see anyone, which makes me conclude that with mighty luck, this place is isolated. The only fortune to gain thus far. With what little adrenaline remains, I hurry up the stairs, hoping it leads to empty rooms.

With every painful step, the ache in my gums intensifies. My hands curl into fists as I force myself not to scream from the suffocating pain. By luck, the first room has a door with only a knob—no sight of a lock in place. I gather my energy to walk right through it, slamming the door shut behind me. Before there is even a chance of getting disgusted by the thought of me standing in a secluded, empty room above a brothel, my legs crumble making me fall to my knees once more. My skin doesn't depict it, but my body is painfully scalding. An invisible fire scorches my skin. Simultaneously, the taste of more blood seeps from my gums when the fangs shoot through, pooling inside my mouth until I spit it out onto the wooden floorboards. Disgusted, I spin away and find myself looking at a cracked old mirror on the wall. A gasp rips from my throat. My skin tone is turning into alabaster, as opposed to my usual Californian sun-kissed tan. My fear heightens when my breathing slows down. Seconds later, my body erupts again in shooting pain, and dear heavens, all I can do now is lie on this filthy floor beneath me, screaming in agony

"Argh! My mouth... my jaw!" I roll from side to side, clutching my stomach until my lungs collapse and my strength all but drained. My body becomes limp, my eyelids groggy as I struggle to keep them open. Before I lose the fight and close my eyes once more, my mother's words come to mind.

Prophecy.

Vampire.

Pain.

Monster.

****

One blood-thirsty week later...

"Oh no, not again!" I clutch my abdomen, feeling another spasm erupt. Fangs elongate and restlessness washes over me as I find myself, once again, craving blood. I tried over the past week, since turning, to avoid drinking, but that only led me to more pain. At one point, the thirst for blood was so overwhelming that the monster in me succumbed to the hunger. It was too dominant. Too desirable to stay away from.

Sating my hunger is also an issue. Those men and frivolous flappers are no longer jovial, as my thirst for blood overtook the thirst for my humanity back. Some tasted like alcohol, and others of lust. But at the end of the day, blood is all I craved. All I desired. Once the emotional roller coaster ended, I realized I needed to leave right away. The last thing I wanted was for the authorities to discover me surrounded by dead bodies. No one should know what I am except me. It is my shameful secret.

As I hide in an alleyway the next block over, the hunger pang hits like a slap in the face. I constantly seem to be tense when this happens, almost unnerved unless I feed. It is quite irritating. My senses are overwhelmingly strong.

Nonetheless, it takes longer to acclimate to the sensations. Even now, the scent of the brunette woman in the distance is intoxicating. I sniff the air, like a dog sniffing out his next meal. The aroma of her blood is so inviting, so deliciously strong, like roses in a garden. I take a whiff of the scent, immediately recognizing the fragrant rose oil mixed with ambrosia, to be exact. The blood coursing through her veins is intense, beckoning me. Even though I know it is wrong, I've passed the point of no return after consuming enough blood that would even make a nurse in a hospital quiver. The monster pulls within, and I cannot seem to fight him. I do not want to be the predator that finds his prey, but there is little choice in the matter, so my hunt begins. Following the scent, I swiftly move. The hunger gets more impatient every second that is wasted. The woman—my prey—that seems to be the one who emanates the scented oils, stands outside the door as if waiting for someone.

"I am so sorry," I whisper out into the enveloping humidity. Then make my move straight toward her.

I am barely a few feet away from her until she whips her head in my direction. Her eyes settle straight on mine. Her expression stuns me as she looks…expectant. Before there is a chance to pounce, a powerful force hits me like a lightning bolt. The energy zaps through me and my body flies backward, forcing me to land on my back. The aggravation of being attacked by my dinner only enforces my hunger. Gnarling at her, my eyes focus on the tall woman wearing a much longer dress than the flappers. Her hair is shoulder length, neatly twirled in a plait. There is little evidence that shows her being of poor status, but not wealthy either. Regardless, these hunger pangs are strong, which lead me to try and pounce again at the woman with a strange power. However, my plan fails as I attempt to get up from the ground, my body suddenly freezes. In the most literal sense, I am frozen in place as the mysterious woman stands over me, giving me a most curious glance. I try to snarl, elongating my fangs, but it does not work, so I narrow my gaze at her instead. I am captured by her mystical eyes as she leans down toward me, sitting on her haunches, not caring about the ends of her long dress getting stained from the ground. The need to move is strong, which further aggravates me in this frozen state. Suddenly, she reaches out her hand toward my face. I notice how slender it is, delicate, covered in the shade of sweet honey.

"I need to know," she whispers as she gingerly takes her index finger and places it on my forehead.

In what feels like a millisecond, she gasps, then suddenly her eyes become white as snow, a contrast to her skin tone. Her finger trembles but stays put against my forehead. With lightning speed, she retracts her hand and then jumps backward, which is the exact reaction I first wanted from her.

Gawking at me, disbelief in her expression, she says, "How can this be?"

I cannot respond except narrow my gaze again, trying not to make it obvious that I am quite confused at her statement. She must realize this and, with a quick wave of her hand, I am released from my frozen state.

She cools her expression of surprise, caught off guard by me for some unknown reason. Our eyes meet and, in a flash, her demeanor changes. "Try nothing, Mr. Phillips. I am stronger than you expected the first time round. Nothing will change the second time, I can assure you of that."

"Who are you? How do you know me?" I huff out.

A serious look flashes across her face as she holds out her hand. "You must come with me. Please, trust me. You are out in a world you know little about, Zachary. It's dangerous for someone so new."

This is certainly not what I expected to happen. Perplexed, yet curious, I accept her hand. She holds on tightly, then helps lift me from the ground. It feels warm yet odd, as I have had no one intentionally touch me in a while. In most cases, I mortify them. They often die quickly after the screaming begins. Frowning at the thought, the woman interrupts my wallowing by letting go and gesturing her head toward the door.

Sensing a strong intuition not to fear her, I follow her into the shop. A wooden chair lies near a table as if it is awaiting my presence, so I take it and sit. Intrigue flows through me, wanting to find out what this woman knows. Neither of us is human, which means she may be quite knowledgeable.

"I'll bring you something to keep you a little sated." She sashays over to her little kitchenette. Anticipation kicks in when I see her return holding a bottle, which appears to be ale at first, but then after accepting it, I take a closer look. Squinting down the bottleneck, the dark red liquid tells me otherwise. So does its intoxicating metallic scent.

An emotion of anxiety courses through me, but I

immediately swallow it, clearing my throat. "You store blood in bottles for all your guests?"

Not too long after asking that question, I realize my disrespect toward her. Did my manners disappear with my last breath?

"Sorry, ma'am. Thank you for your help. I must apologize for my behavior... I am finding it hard to keep this monster at bay. The thirst is never-ending. If it had been under any other circumstances, I would never wish for your harm."

The woman cackles, giving me a baffled look. "Zachary, first, please call me Stella. Second, I have more strength than you can imagine, so you would have never reached me. To answer your first question, over time I have made a few vampire acquaintances, so I try to offer them what they prefer to drink. Wouldn't you agree that sounds favorable? More hospitable?" She smiles as I accept the bottle, giving her a nod in agreement.

Stella then turns around and walks over to a table with a pack of cards that are placed amongst a round blue ball that sits in the middle of it. I peer over at the bottle. My gaze settles over her mannerisms, including the way she mumbles to herself. I have heard of people like her, but they were folk tales of women and men who liked to peek into the souls of townspeople, trying to see into their futures. Some considered the fortune-telling was correct, yet many people thought it to be shenanigans of crazed people or, depending on how you perceive it—smart ones who fooled people into giving them their money. But with what I saw outside, there was no room for uncertainty about her power. Even if magic has never been something I believed.

I raise an eyebrow. "Do I want to know how you source the blood?"

With a devilish smile, Stella rests her hand on her curvaceous hip. "That would depend on how much of your humanity you are dangling on by."

Humanity. The word that I must keep on referring to. I pause at her comment, looking down at the bottle only inches away from my mouth. The blood in front of me is calling, a hunger too strong for me to deny it. I pick up the bottle, peer down at the red thick liquid, then quickly gulp it down. The tang takes time to get accustomed to but my thirst for it overpowers all rationality.

Goodness, how can I despise drinking this yet yearn for it like a possessed man?

"I guess that's your answer," says Stella as she watches, throwing curious glances at me. Feeling uncomfortable with the looks she gives me, I wipe my mouth with the cuff of my sleeve. "How do you know my name? I never spoke a word to you before, yet you know not only my name but what I am."

She clasps her hands, then gestures to me to sit by her at the small timber table. I walk over and take a seat, cocking an eyebrow as I wait for an answer.

"I am a witch with a third eye. To translate, I can see into the future. This means I can foresee a person's presence. For example, you may assume that we met by circumstance. However, it was, in fact, expected. I foresaw you getting weak, which meant you were thirsty for blood, or not consumed enough of it. Knowing this, I stood outside, waiting for you to approach me. I knew you were a freshly turned vampire and found it a necessity to protect my town. After all, we are prey for your kind."

"But you looked stunned when you gazed into my eyes…"

Stella taps her chin and then nods. "Yes, I did. Even though I knew who you were well before we met, I was not aware of how important you are until I peered into your future. Occasionally, it is a clearer vision when I make contact with the person. On this occasion, to touch the person. You still don't comprehend what you are, or how to live in our world."

Admittingly, I am chilled by the revelation of how she foresaw me attacking her, as well as the depth of her knowledge of who I am.

"I… I am still unsure of what to do or how to live with… all of this." I point at my gums as I extract my fangs. The way Stella watches me as I open up to her unsettles me which makes me rub the back of my neck, a habit that has stuck with me since I became immortal.

"On my journey from leaving my home… well, everything changed, and I became this monster… The pain was torturous. Still is sometimes."

My mother was right when she said it would be a pain I had never felt before.

Stella waves her hand to silence me, which I admit works. "Do not dwell on what has happened to you already. You transformed, even though painful, it happened, so, you must now understand the world you live in. You walk amongst the living, whether they are humans or other paranormal beings. Don't dismiss it or pretend it's not real. It is." Adjusting the unruly curls in her long-plaited hair, she continues. "You are of significant importance for the future. You will have a role in saving lives, when though, is still unclear.

Something will happen one day, Zachary, which means you would need to prepare yourself for change. To make a significant choice in your immortal life."

If I ever had a time when my mind was in disarray, this moment would outshine the others. I never felt this unsure, scared, angry before. Especially so hungry.

I do my best to swallow my fear, then say, "What do I need to know? What should I do? My mother babbled on about me being the future Vampire King… If you know more, please, I would appreciate your help. A supply of more blood too, if possible, otherwise the monster inside will find another means of eating. Truth be told, I hate doing it."

Stella looks me in the eye and purses her lips. I can see she is thinking, the cogs turning in her head.

"Connor. He is the one you must seek to find your answers." Her spoken words are cryptic, which grates my nerves. "For now, you can stay with me. The last thing we need are flappers flopping like flies with holes in their necks." She laughs as she shakes her head, amused at the thought.

I give a quick nod, but on the inside, my anxiety reels its way up, leaving my heart pounding. Not to mention that my fangs are aching to shoot through my already swollen gums. But it's not for hunger. Instead, it's anger and aggravation. So much has transpired in a short time that my emotions are chaotic.

"So much is happening. I feel foolish for not believing my mother, or for not prying enough for more questions," I exasperate.

Stella stands up and grabs my shoulder, the grip harder than I expect. I am blinded by her white pupils, staring right at mine.

"Zachary, you cannot be angry about something you knew nothing about. From a human's perspective, you have to see that at the time you were one, they considered tales of a vampire's sheer madness. Everyone who wasn't a believer laughed at the concept. Your reaction was just that. But now you must accept the change and forget your past. You must think of your present, as well as your future, that is all."

All I can do is nod in agreement, but then pause as a thought comes to me. I shrug my shoulders, looking at her with loss. "What do I do? How can I live in this dark world with little to no knowledge of it?"

Stella plants her slender hands on her hips, smirking at me. "Well then, if you calm down, please take a seat. I will tell you."

****

It's been two days since I met Stella, and here I am laying on her couch where I have been sleeping. I feel like a moocher, but I have nowhere else to go. Stella is gracious enough to offer to share her space with me. Her words are like a broken record in my mind.

"You cannot dismiss this future, or your world now. Stay in the shadows, don't make friends. If you find it difficult to find a human source, then you may resort to animals. However, do not drink from animals that have a gray aura, even when you are starving. It is a sign the animal is infected, or ill. Now, it's clear that the plague is very infectious in humans. You are lucky to have not caught it prior, but that doesn't mean you can't feel unwell from the blood of a diseased animal or person. Even though no disease can kill you, avoid consuming certain blood. Do you understand what I mean?"

I give a quick nod, which seems to mean the end of the topic as Stella jumps to the next subject—drinking blood.

"If you need to drink, then you must do what you need to do to get the sustenance you require because it will strengthen you as well as keep you sane. It's your nature now, but be mindful of whom you drink from, particularly how you do it. Your senses are heightened now. You should be able to sense ill health in a human. This will help you choose victims. You must stop before their heart does. You will notice it whilst you drink, and when you force yourself to stop, you must lick their wounds to avoid it scarring them. Remember, the last thing we need is for humans to learn about our world or what we can do. It is a code that all paranormal creatures abide by."

It feels like my mind is working on double time as I do my best to absorb everything that is now part of my life. I'm suddenly snapped back out of my reverie.

"Are you ready for today?"

My eyes snap open, finding Stella leaning against the wall, hand resting on her hip, her face holding a serious expression. I even see a hint of concern.

I stretch my arms over my head, then sit up, throwing my legs over the couch. My fingers rake through my hair as I shrug. "Yes, and no… What if it turns out to be just a waste of time? I do not know this Connor. What if I make a mockery of myself by announcing I need his help, especially that I am the future king? It still sounds like baloney in my mind, despite the many times you told me otherwise."

With a sigh, Stella walks over then sits beside me. She shifts her body toward me, gives me a wary look, then frowns as she says, "I had a vision yesterday which I chose not to divulge but I think you should know. It's about Connor and you—"

"No, please. No more. I don't want to know any new visions of yours. You said I need to meet this man, that he may guide me or tell me more about my future. Besides, it is not all about learning this but finding a place for me. I can't stay in Los Angeles any longer. It feels like living in a nightmare, but all I need is…freedom. A home."

As I finish my pleading, I notice Stella's lips are thin, her frown not leaving her face. "You shouldn't dismiss every undesirable thing you hear, Zachary. You scorned your mother over her revelation, and now you are dismissing me. But, if that is what you want to do, then I cannot force you to listen." She then passes me a torn piece of paper with an address written on it along with the directions on how to get there. "Here, you'll need this."

I take the paper and tuck it into my pocket. Getting up, I walk over to my duffel bag sitting on the wooden table, all packed with my essentials, including a few bottles of blood to keep me sated on the way. I put it over my shoulder then turn to Stella, who is still sitting on the couch, watching me. Her expression looks torn. I suspect it's about what she wanted to talk to me about. But I just want to get out of here and not waste another minute. I need a new life, and if there is a possibility this Connor can help me, then I have nothing to lose.

"Thank you, Stella, for helping me despite how I chose you to be my snack," I say with a smirk, trying to cheer her up after my sour dismissal.

Stella gives a playful smirk. "You're welcome, but

just for you to know, you wouldn't have had the chance to get close to me, anyway. Besides, you were pleasant company." The smirk transforms into a genuine smile, giving her face a youthful appearance as opposed to what she would look like in human years. Probably a corpse. I don't ask her age, as I find it forthcoming, which may be offensive. Although, I know that it's much, much older than my measly one week. Just as I turn toward the door, she grasps my arm. "Oh, wait, I forgot to give you something."

I narrow my eyes, trying to determine what else she could need to give me, other than the extra bottles of blood.

Stella disappears into her bedroom, then shortly reappears, holding what shocks me. A Lewis Automatic Pistol, a gun that I never had expected Stella to carry, nor own.

"What are you doing with that?"

"It's for you... I keep it with me in case I get attacked by vampires, but my power is growing stronger, so I no longer fear them. But for you, I thought it would be helpful to have in case you get attacked and need a way out. Before you ask me how a gun kills a vampire, the answer is, it won't. But this gun has bullets that I have cursed to turn into a point of a stake as they hit the skin of a vampire. If you aim into their hearts, it will only then affect them. Otherwise, it'll just be pesky for them. Besides, it's not that difficult to get hold of. With all the firearms being sold at black markets these days, not everything can be one hundred percent regulated." She finishes with a snicker.

I stand in place, surprised by this situation, but find my hand accepting the disturbing gift.

"Good. You give me no need to quarrel with you about this. Take the pistol but be discreet with it, hiding it in a place where no one will discover it. Only use it if you need to. Not using it correctly can do you more harm than it can to others. Perhaps Connor can teach you how to use it." She finishes quietly.

The thought confuses me, though. Why would Connor help at all? But the thought disappears when her hands land on my shoulders, squeezing them. "Be careful, Zachary. Remember, do not make your current state known to anyone, even to non-humans. Stay quiet and keep questions to yourself, only until you meet Connor." She then gives me a tight hug, catching me off guard, but I linger a little longer, liking the warmth of another body after not being hugged in such a long time. When she finally lets go, I say, "Thank you, Stella, I will not forget your kindness."

Giving her a lopsided grin, I open the door. With my duffel bag on my shoulder, I turn my head away from Stella then walk out into the warm Californian afternoon.

Chapter Three

ZACHARY

Santa Monica

The thrumming of nerves tells me how I feel about meeting this Connor person. Stella never elaborated who he was or the reason it was important to meet him, leaving me at the deep end. I decide the ideal thing to do is to catch the train to Santa Monica. Luckily, I remembered to take some money before leaving home, which made it all the easier to purchase a train ticket and head to Santa Monica.

The train ride itself is quick despite being uncomfortable, thanks to bumpy tracks. Getting off the train, I look down at the folded piece of paper in my sweaty palm, re-reading the address.

Turning my head around as I stand on the platform, my eyes land on the conductor. His demeanor shows he is disinterested, as if he just wants to continue his shift without being bothered. I quickly shuffle over to him, regardless.

"Pardon me, I hope you could point out the directions," I show him the paper as I point to the address.

The conductor glances down at the writing and his eyes widen as his Latin-colored skin turns a lighter shade. He springs back from me as the bored demeanor he wears shifts rapidly. He begins speaking in Spanish, as he makes the sign of the cross across his body. I sense his pulse quickening, feeling his fear rolling off in waves. His heartbeat makes me salivate. I lick my lips but then rip my gaze back to his eyes, doing my best to stay strong as his pulse calls to me. This hunger is becoming constant, which baffles me, as I should be sated enough after finishing the bottles that Stella gave me, plus an unanticipated snack in my carriage. What a frightening scene when someone opens that bathroom door.

Rubbing my temples, hating the image of the man slumped on the floor. Yet, I remember how warm the blood tasted as it poured down my throat. The imagery is conflicting. How now I live as a creature that is immortal and evil, yet it leaves me sinking in an entire sea of clashing emotions.

The conductor stares at me, as I haven't made a move since my thought process went onto a hungry tangent. Straightening my posture, I speak what little Spanish I know, doing my best to reassure him I am all right, that there is nothing to be afraid of. To my surprise, he responds in broken English, eyeing me warily as he tries to keep his distance. He gives me directions, as I kindly requested.

I walk for a mile until my eyes rest on the building. From afar, the vastness of it is wondrous, well superseding my home, despite it considered quite large to all the other neighbors around us. By the looks of this building, our wealth was minuscule. The decor intertwined in the exterior is transfixing and eye-catching. My gaze trails around the gardens, then settles on the house of bricks hidden beneath the paint. The color reminds me of a blush that stains a woman's cheek.

Finally, I have arrived.

I walk toward the door, which sits atop five steps. The last step brings me face to face with a large, framed wood, its enormity intimidating me without seeing what's behind it. I finally lift the door knocker, feeling the cold yet smooth brass against my hand, then knock it three times.

However, I am greeted with silence.

Perseverance, Zachary, perseverance.

My hand lifts once more but never reaches the door knocker as it suddenly opens. The loud creak grating me. An elderly man appears in front of me, his appearance giving me the impression that he must be the butler.

I straighten my shoulders, remembering the importance of posture, and try to follow the etiquette I have heard the wealthier folk do, or at least the nagging of Mother, when she cared for me.

The man looks back at me, expecting more than just a lonesome man staring at an old butler. I clear my throat. "Good evening, sir. I have traveled to meet with a gentleman called Connor. I have been told this is his residence and would be pleased to speak with him."

The butler glances over his shoulder, which I assume means he is waiting for permission to invite me inside. Finally, with a nod, he turns back to me. "Follow me. He is expecting you." A simple sentence yet still gives me the chills if that's even feasible for a vampire. I nod in what I hope seems like an appreciative gesture, as he grabs hold of the doorknob opening it wider for entrance.

Stepping inside to follow him, my footsteps clack against the marble floor, leaving an echo throughout the lobby. However, it stops once I am brought to the door.

He gestures toward it then knocks on my behalf.

"Enter," is all the response I get, which causes me to swallow deeply, making me wish I could drink a bottle of blood before getting the courage to see this man.

I run my fingers through my hair a few times before I bring up the nerve to open the door. Turning the knob, the door opens wide, and my eyes become glued to this man, leaning against a table, long arms resting across his chest. He exudes confidence, with a sense of worldliness.

But what really strikes me are his features. Shoulder-length black hair that appears to be tied back, with dark green eyes which hold me in place. He has a tall frame, with his nose and jaw in perfect symmetry. He exudes power in his posture. I then notice a small cleft in his chin, which reminds me of my own. The only difference left is our attire. He wears a clean suit, the complete opposite of what I look like. I realize that I haven't worn something neat in a while. I can't remember when I last had a warm bath or fresh clothing.

"For all that's unholy in this world, you are truly identical to me," the man says as he rubs his chin, looking at me with curiosity. Possibly even wonder.

"H-how? What?" was all that I can muster, still reeling with confusion. So far, my excited disposition had diminished, as this wasn't what I expected to discover. Not even close.

"Ah, look at your expression, brother, priceless!"

he says in an amused tone. If only I could match his ease and amusement, perhaps my demeanor would have been different. But hearing him say *brother*? That's beyond what I had ever expected.

"I don't…understand. How can we be identical? How do you know about me?" I throw out the words, the questions, the shock.

Connor's lips thin as he narrows his gaze. "I understand you being so perplexed, I was, too. I only found out a week ago." Then he shrugs and gestures toward a chair by the table.

I take a seat, waves of bewilderment running through me at the prospect of sitting opposite my long-lost twin brother. My hands are still clammy as I run them against my pants, eager to learn about the secrets he holds.

"I will make it simple for you. I am your brother. As you are aware, we are identical, too." My eyes widen at the news, and I open my mouth to question him more, but he lifts his hands up. "Before you fire away more questions," he says, rolling his eyes, "the reason you weren't aware of me was because on the night we were born, I was taken away. You see, the Vampire Council ensured our mother was compelled into believing she had only one baby," he says as he chuckles. "Humans are so feeble-minded and weak."

Dismissing the human comment, I lean forward, my expression no doubt with wonder. "Why? Why would someone do such an atrocious thing as taking away a baby from his mother?" The tone in my voice grows cold toward the atrocity.

Connor quickly puts his hand up in a silencing gesture. "No need to fear or fume. The leader of the

Vampire Council motioned I needed to be taken from my birth mother. It was the only way to bring me up as a leader. He did it for the better, as according to him, the legend is that I am to become the Vampire King. The first in over a millennium, so you can see why it was important to leave a mediocre human family in South Los Angeles. I can only thank the man that brought me up here," Connor says as he gazes at the room we're in. I look around too, following his gaze, taking in its awe. Swiveling my head around as I notice paintings scattered across the walls, the elegance of tasteful furniture situated all over the large room. It feels royal, yet ancient. I can only picture it as a castle that was restored to fit in with the 1920s California. Not too long after eying the room, my nose gets a little twitchy as I pick up on a scent. I then realize that even though my surroundings are beautiful, it gives off a dreary sense of death. In fact, it reeks of it.

"Did you ever want to meet your parents even if you appreciate the man that stole you from her?" I blurt.

He cocks an eyebrow at me. "That's what you ask after I tell you I am the Vampire King? About pathetic humans? Me wanting to meet you?" He makes an incredulous laugh, as if the questions I ask are comedic.

"Zachary, firstly, I found out about you the night I turned. My mentors explained it, then proceeded to tell me an all-too-long explanation of my past, present, and future. Sorry, brother, but I have little to no interest in your life. I am bred to rule. You are simply,"—he pauses and then snaps his finger— "an anomaly in the Prophecy." I reel back slightly, not expecting the menace in his tone.

Suddenly, my throat clogs up, and my vocal cords strain. I am too shocked to even respond to such malice. A vision of Mother yelling at me as she lay ill, words of pain thrown as hard as a hailstorm pelting against the window. Now I feel like it's happening all over again.

He knows so much, yet I am just hearing this news. Suddenly I lose my parents, then only now find out that I have an identical twin who all too quickly rejects me as if I am a leper. Again and again, I am knocked back by the illusion of familial love. However, I bite back my depressing perception of family. "How do you know of the Prophecy? Why do you think I am some magical,"—I wave my hand in the air, trying to find the right words, then blurt out—"blunder?"

"Why, Zachary? Because I am the Vampire King. I am the Prophecy."

"But Mother said I'll be the Vampire King…"

As quick as a flash, Connor is suddenly inches away from my face with his hands fisting my collar.

His voice is deep, dripping with power as he says, "*I* am the Vampire King. That parasite of a human was wrong. She was a human, a chosen birth canal for a strong vampire. In the end, it psychologically broke her."

I try to shrug away from him but to no avail. He is stronger than me, even if he has only been a vampire for as long as I. "I don't mean you any harm. Please, let me go. I just came here to find… to meet you."

"Well, we've met. So now, there is nothing else here for you," he says as he lets go of my collar, but with such force that my backside almost slips off the chair. His insolence shocks me, leaving me with my mouth wide open. At first, I am too shocked for words, but eventually, I find them.

"Is that all? We just reunited. You're not giving me a chance to…to…" Pursing my lips, I calm down, then start again. "I have nowhere to go, Connor. You are literally the only family I have left, yet, you're not even willing to get to know me. Not even an ounce of interest? Are you worried I appeared out of nowhere purely to overthrow you, or do you think of me as a four-flusher? At least have the decency to tell me why you are turning me away?" My tone gets slightly louder, despite doing my best to keep my growing anger at bay.

Connor rolls his eyes as he walks back over to the table, taking a seat, his posture straight, almost as if he was aristocratic.

"The Vampire Council brought me up. They adhere to the visions of what an oracle told them about the Prophecy, which led me to grow into this…" He shrugs his shoulders nonchalantly, then looks at me with a gleam. "All there is to know about the vampire species, what's expected, and how to play the role that my destiny set out. I don't need friends or a family. They are enough for me. Plus, the delectable women. Can't forget to mention them." A sly smirk appears, which sickens me.

He enjoys it. He isn't like me, he is worse. Maybe it's better to stay away from him than get too close.

"Oh, also, in regard to me worrying that you want to be king is quite amusing because, Zachary, you wouldn't get far. From what I can see, you don't look like anything more than a commoner. Let me guess, and correct me if I am wrong, but do you still find it disgusting every time you drink? Or feel guilty before attacking a human so you can quench the painful hunger pangs? Does your conscious talk to you?"

My jaw falls open as I process his questions. I fall into his intimidation, finding myself nodding. Yes, to all those questions.

I wish the circumstance is different, where I could deny it. To be the big dangerous vampire. He seems to fit the image. Instead, I feel weak in the bones, pained and betrayed by my own blood. Even if I just found out about him. My lips do not move, not even an attempt. I'm speechless as he really has me stuck in a corner.

"I see my assumptions are correct." Conner grins as he comes to the correct conclusion, then crosses his leg over the other, a smug expression growing. I can see it in his eyes, too. He's enjoying this moment, which quickly makes my anger rise.

"My feelings toward the situation are my own. I will learn to deal with them. The entire reason for me coming here was to get some answers, but now discovering we are of the same blood, I want... more." My stomach churns as I speak, and more for what comes out next. "To be the Vampire King is not of interest. Instead, all I truly want is a family. Not to live alone in a world that sucks the life out of people." Standing up, I adjust my jacket. "Perhaps we could come to an agreement? Let me stay and learn from you. There will be no mention of the possibility of me even becoming King. If you want me in the dark shadows, hidden away, then I can oblige."

I notice a curious glint in his eyes as he rubs his cleft chin. The seconds tick by until he says, "And hypothetically, if I were to allow you to stay here, what would that entail?"

"You could provide me with my own quarters. I will leave you be, keeping to myself. Perhaps over time, you could explain to me everything you know. I have not much knowledge of this life. Let's just say, curiosity gets the best of me." A chuckle leaves my mouth unexpectedly, considering the topic is serious.

The expression on Connor's face shows not an ounce of amusement, yet he rises from the chair, stalking closer to me. He glances down at my arm stretched out toward him, encouraging a handshake and, for a second there, I imagine the gun that Stella gave. It feels like I am the prey, with the gun being my only weapon from the predator coming toward me.

"Mmm, well, I have a better plan. You can stay on my terms." His smile grows as he waits for me to question further. I feel nervous that he has come up with his own terms.

"And what are those terms?" I ask, defeated.

"You stay. But you can never leave."

That's outrageous!

"What do you mean, never leave?" Worry increases as I wait.

Connor taps his bottom lip and then says, "Until the Prophecy is fulfilled."

"I don't even know what actually happens in the Prophecy myself. How can I know when it is fulfilled?"

Connor doesn't respond, just shrugs. "I need my mate, my future Queen. We must bind once united. That's all I'll discuss for now."

This arrogant man who shares my blood is turning out to be selfish. His expression screams 'devious'. Do I really want to tangle in his web?

"Well? My terms, or you leave. Choose. I'm not a

patient creature, Zachary."

"Agreed," he slips out before I have the chance to realize the consequences. That one word echoes through my mind. Then it hits me, but too late. I realize I have just condemned myself to hell.

"Good. It is settled then." He rubs his hands together. "You shall be given a room. My rules must be followed, just like every other vampire does. You keep to your own business, and if anyone ever asks why you look like me or vice versa, the answer should be that a witch cursed you to look identical to me—" He pauses, then grins.— "because you were so hideous to look at." Connor's devilish grin widens as he enjoys hearing his ridiculous concoction. I open my mouth to respond, but he shoves a hand in my face, a rude gesture to let me know he isn't finished yet. "You will learn more about this lifestyle, follow my instructions. I think I will also utilize you for business purposes. You might come in handy one day. It's also best to remind you to expect nothing more of our shared blood. You're not family, Zachary, just an anomaly in an ancient vision."

My Adam's apple bobs as I swallow my retort, never knowing such anger toward someone he had never met, albeit his own flesh and blood.

Yet, I know with his importance, it can be helpful for me in this world. One day, I know I'll walk out of this nightmare a stronger creature. A free creature. But my humanity? Well, that I will hold onto as best as I can.

Chapter Four

IVY

Santa Monica, 2018

"I'm so disappointed in you both! All I want is to do is study part-time at the Santa Monica School of Dance and Music, then teach dance. But your desire for me to become a frickin' doctor is insane. How can you make me do something that I'm not passionate about? Is it money? I will pay you back, guys, I promise." By this point, I am all over the place, going on about their unwanted opinions. Nothing seems to stop me from keeping my mouth shut as I shout vehemently at them. "I don't understand why you simply won't support me in my career!"

I'm trying to contain my anger, tears flowing like a waterfall down my face. It's a low point for me because this isn't the way they brought me up. To speak to them this way is very out of character.

"Ivy, you don't understand. You need to learn how to deal with blood or anything that leads to a bloody situation. Y-you can't run from it. Or dance away from it! If you can become a doctor or a paramedic, or at least a profession where you'll work with blood on a daily basis. This would help you be a little prepared for the future." My mother begs, her eyes pleading, hoping for me to understand what she means. But I have absolutely no idea what she is talking about. Unfortunately, this is when my stubbornness takes over again.

I snap at them, throwing my hands in the air dramatically. "I don't know what you want from me! What parent wants their child to deal with gory shit? Most would say, 'go out there, follow your dreams', or 'we don't agree but we will support you', not literally tell me to work with death!"

I fume at how they refuse to pay for the education I want. They know I fear needles. The cherry on top of this shitty idea of a career for me is that I find blood disgusting. It's hate at first sight.

My dad sits on the couch opposite me. His arms cross against his chest as he exhales a heavy breath, watching us argue. I glance over at him, noticing him grab hold of Mom's hand. "Now, now, let's calm down and talk about this rationally. Heather, sweetheart, we need to explain to her why we want her to study something different. You're being way too vague, and it's just going to confuse Ivy more." He looks at me. "Ivy, calm down, please. Just listen to us. Trust me, we have a reason for all of this."

But no, I've had enough of the topic, not interested in hearing what their reasoning is.

"Whatever, I'm gonna go… I need some space from the both of you." I admit, my voice hitches a little as I suppress more tears. My eyes are now bloodshot red as my hand continuously wipes away the tears.

"Ivy, wait! Please, listen to us!" Whilst my head is in a world of its own, I still as my father strides after me, speaking in a tone that I've never heard before. "Ivy, there is no way you can leave at a time like this.

We may seem ridiculous at times, trust me, we are very aware of your embarrassment of us, but this" —he pauses as he gestures toward my mom, then sighs— "is serious. We can't fluff around about it. There is something you need to know about because it relates to your future. Please, sweetheart, come sit down with us so we can explain the reason we worry about you wanting to pursue a career in dance."

Reluctantly, my feet move toward the couch, and I sit back down directly opposite them. Sighing, I run my hand through my hair. "Guys, please just tell me what this is all about because I am pissed off. I don't really feel like pretending to be happy right now."

Mom speaks first, wringing a towel in her hands. To say she was nervous is an understatement. "Well, it started the night we conceived you. I had a dream—"

My dad interrupts her rambling. "*We* had a dream, actually. It was the same dream for both of us. That's what made us scared and confused."

"Okay, weird, yes, but what's the point of this?" I raise my eyebrows.

Mom exhales but keeps herself composed. "It was pitch black. The darkness engulfed us, then a woman's voice filled my—our—heads. It was soft, but clear. She said that the child in my belly will be powerful. That it will have a significant part in leading the vampires. Even in the dream, I wanted to laugh at how preposterous it sounded, but then an image flashed…it showed you screaming in pain, with fangs—"

And ladies and gentlemen, my parents have officially lost their minds.

I stand abruptly before she could utter any other nonsense. "Look, I appreciate you want to talk to me, but you need to understand that you both sound absurd. Now, I just really, *really* want to be on my own. I think I'll head down to the Pier and… clear my head. This is way too much. I don't want to deal with this right now. It's unjustified. No wacky dream of yours is a logical reason."

I turn but stop midway to look at them. Straightening my posture, with my head held up high. "Now I'm eighteen, whilst I may not be legal to drink, I am old enough to make my own decisions. I will pursue my dreams of dancing. I will go to the Santa Monica School of Dance and Music, with or without your approval."

And move out as soon as I can too.

I hold my cell phone in one hand and use the other to quickly grab my purple bag. I do a hurried search within and nod to myself, satisfied with the items stuffed inside. My leotard, ballet shoes, and wallet. Without a second glance, I then walk out the door, needing to escape the tension that fills my home.

As I walk down the footpath toward my car, a cute red Kia Soul that my parents bought for my birthday, I unlock it with a push of a button.

Yet as every step is closer to freedom, I get an uneasy sensation in my stomach.

****

The sun is glaring, with the humidity disgustingly suffocating—it feels like a noose around my throat. I don't mind the hot weather, but not when it's muggy. Looking over at the small crowd in the middle of the Pier, I spot Damien in the middle.

I grin at the sight. Of course, he's always surrounded by a crowd when he plays the guitar.

He is the pure depiction of a beach babe—tanned, blond hair that reminds me of the wet sand. I even refer to him as my beach boyfriend. Of course, it's all platonic, but I joke about him using that description.

I migrate toward the group of people, standing amongst them, content to have his music lift my mood.

The song finishes just as my shoulders fall, finally relaxed. He grins, and gestures for me to come over to him. I roll my eyes dramatically as he beckons me, but a grin surpasses my playfulness. I walk over, enjoying the attention as the crowd of hawkers dissipates.

Damien makes his way closer to me and then envelopes me in a warm hug. "Heya, Ives, was wondering when you'd appear."

I hug him tightly, smelling the faint scent of suncream. "Oh, aren't you so sure of yourself? Well, just to burst your ego bubble, I actually didn't know you were here." I pause, giving him a smirk then childishly stick out my tongue.

Damien chuckles as he squats down and places his guitar back into its case. "Okay, so to what do I owe this honor?"

I take a deep exhale, needing to clear my mind in order to have a clear explanation for my mood, before I blurt out the discussion—okay, argument—with my parents. But all the tension returns, then verbal diarrhea ensues. Damien stands up, concern visible in his eyes, and hovers close to me, his sandy eyebrows drawn as he listens to me recap the scenario.

As soon as I finish, a sigh leaves me, as if it feels better to talk about it. Although I still feel pissed off, but at least I have someone to vent to. He too understands familial issues, but his are worse. His dad is a mean son of a bitch, tough as hell. I know Damien respects him, but there is also fear too.

"Come, Ivy, let's sit down." He points toward an empty bench. We walk over and I swiftly plonk my bag onto the floor, then sit down.

"Far out, Damien. What do I do? I hate fighting. Especially disappointing people. It's an annoying personality trait of mine," I mutter.

Damien wraps his arm around my shoulders. "It's not annoying, Ives. Listen, it's normal for families to have disagreements. It just depends on how you manage them. Like, you can learn to accept they don't view your career as important as you do, but it doesn't mean you never speak to them. It also may not mean you can't save money by working part time, or choosing to study whatever you want to, regardless of their opinion."

"Mmm," is all I say as I consider his words.

"The dream part is a bit freaky, though. Not sure what your mom is talking about. I think she's taking a nightmare seriously," Damien adds.

I cackle at his obvious comment. "Ya think? Gosh, she sounded ridiculous."

Damien laughs, unwrapping his arms from me and leans back against the bench.

I cross my legs, feeling the warmth of the sun on them as I stare out at the view. The horizon is so clear, the water magnificent, with people running on the sand. It's not as busy as usual, which I don't find surprising with this annoying heat wave. Most people are in pools or thanking the amazing person who created the air conditioner.

"Maybe I should quit. Go back to wanting to study

philanthropy instead," I spit out.

It's something I was interested in at one point, but my fascination and, well, for a lack of a better word, obsession with dancing took over that aspiration.

Damien clicks his fingers, chuckling at my comment. "Yes, I remember that! You wanted to save the world. Ivy the Hero. You wanted to be so many things, all resulted in you,"—he gestures with his fingers as bunny ears— "helping the world to be a better place." He rolls his eyes.

"Whatever, it was inspiring at the time, but now I want to focus on dancing—"

"It's more practical, realistic. Easier to accomplish," Damien cuts in with his perception.

I want to growl, but I smile instead. He loves my dancing, even without complimenting me, it's the way he always pushes me toward it whenever I get discouraged. Just like now. He is my main support network.

I honestly don't know what I would do without him.

My thoughts slowly fade away as I sit with Damien, although a word filters through my brain. Did my parents really say fangs? I shudder at the thought, shaking my head at the disturbing dream.

Shake it off, Ivy. It's all rubbish.

Chapter Five

ZACHARY

Santa Monica, 2021

It's amazing how time flies by. Even though eternity can feel like a drag, it still amazes me at how much has happened since first setting foot on Santa Monica's soil. Not forgetting the steps that lead me to the hell that is Connor's estate.

Like déjà vu, I now stand outside the same door I knocked on ninety-seven years ago. The wood now polished with a wash of white paint over it, as opposed to the original red oak. Staring at the door knocker, anger stirs inside me, hating the VK design. My eyes roll at the sight, something that has since become automatic at anything Vampire King related.

My fist hits the oak. "Such bullshit." My eyes glaze over the wooden door, hoping it sustains a dent or any damage. But no, the door is as solid as it was back in 1924.

I spent the day with the Council, listening to their boring political discussions on the current shenanigans of rogue vampires. That includes watching how everyone kisses Connor's feet. Nothing changed between us as I had once hoped. As time went by, hope turned into a sour thought of why I put myself in this situation. Decades turned into regret, then into downright anger. Sure, my body bulked up, developed myself a six-pack of abs too. My choice in hairstyle changed as well, finding a much simpler hairstyle than my long tresses. But even though I assimilated into the twenty-first century, it was mainly due to the need to look as different from Connor as possible. His looks had changed little except for his taste in his meals. They now include men.

But a change in his taste buds aside, I can still see myself when I look at him. It only leads me resenting being his twin even more. He is a guise of a man, but behind it is the devil with fangs.

As time went by, not just my hair changed but my mood too, now that I think about it. My appearance depicts it too, all broody at times, or at least that's what Stella says when she sees me.

I spin on my feet, eager to leave this hell. This is something I do nightly. Head out for a walk to avoid being anywhere near the Council, or Connor. Or his meals. I just want to be away from all the drama that ensues within the estate.

The twinkling laser lights at the Santa Monica Pier from a distance are so picturesque, depicting how they've certainly enhanced with technology as time went by. The night's breeze surrounds me, and I find it refreshing to step outside, to breathe in the fresh air. My senses pick up immediately as I inhale the evaporated salt water from the beach. The sounds of people laughing, sipping coffee, sound of their shoes dancing on the promenade, all but brightens my mood. The humanity left in me seeps out in reminders to look around, to think of nicer things than bitter thoughts. I rub my temples as I begin my way down the steps. My aim is to do my usual route around the Pier regardless of it being a lengthy walk. My boots barely make the fifth step when I feel a vibration in my back pocket. I don't need to check the name as I know who it is.

My lips move into a grin as I tap the green button on my cell phone.

"To what do I owe this pleasure, Stella?" I say as a smile forms on my mouth. Something that doesn't often happen.

A laugh rings out on the other end. "Well, hello to you too, Zach. It's still so weird how you always know it's me. I'm the Seer here. That's my job!" Her personality had become somewhat more eccentric, but I guess immortality would make you slightly crazy as time went by. Even more for Stella because she could see into the future when a vision calls to her.

I chuckle at her words, relaxed to hear her voice after the unease of being stuck inside the estate. "It's not like I expected to have a psychic bond with you. Besides, you were the one that gave me your blood, letting me drink it without mentioning to me it was yours. That little detail you failed to mention somehow linked your psychic sense to me."

"Semantics, Zachary."

I can imagine her hands waving me away, as she had done many times throughout our friendship.

To this day, Connor isn't aware of our friendship, not that he'd care. But she is my private life, so I want her as safe as possible, even if she acts like she is indestructible.

"So, what did you want to speak to me about, Stella?" I ask, as my eyebrows rise in intrigue.

"Well, you know how you want to break free from

the agreement with Connor?" she asks. It's all I wanted since I realized how much of a mistake it was to remain here. To immerse myself in his twisted, violent world. "Well, I had a vision. I saw her! It's the perfect plan, Zach!"

Woah, what is she talking about?

"Thanks for reminding me about the stupid deal. I don't get who 'she' is, though. You have to tell me more. Now you have my full attention."

Stella huffs and says, "This is going to blow your mind. She's the Queen. The pawn. Your bait!" I can hear her eagerness clear as day.

Bait? Well, if Connor wants a Queen, guess there is no harm in me delivering her.

I put my game face on, ready for the details. "Okay, I'm all ears. How do I go about this?"

Stella's tone goes quiet, which piques my curiosity. "That's another part I need to speak to you about. An incident happened involving her. Or, technically, is happening at this moment."

I glance around, knowing the exact spots where the cameras are located. "Stella, hold on a second," I whisper as I quickly pick up the pace to move further away from the door. I quietly make my way toward a section of garden hidden behind the large, leafy trees surrounding the estate. Finally, I find a suitable spot without a camera and resume the conversation.

"Okay, you have my attention." My voice is now low, the tone serious as I wait to hear more.

"Well, remember when I first met you, I said that you will have a role in saving lives? That something will happen one day, and you will need to prepare yourself for change?" I nod, even though she wasn't there to see it. Of course, I remember it. It was cryptic as all hell, and I didn't know what to do with that information.

"Yes, I recall the conversation, but what does this incident have anything to do with me?"

"You know the Prophecy? Well, this relates to it. The future Queen... she's just transformed, but there has been some 'wolfy' drama that will get out of hand if someone doesn't intervene. This is what I vaguely saw happening. You could save her before they attack, especially in her weakened state. Then aim at bringing her to the estate, offering her up for your freedom from Connor as well as the Vampire Council."

I reach the back of my neck and rub it, frustrated how my night turned a different direction to what I thought it would. All I wanted was some peace to myself.

And then I realize another obstacle in my path.

"What do I do about Connor?"

There was no response for a few seconds before she finally exhaled.

"Lie to him, Zach. He isn't the good guy in my vision. Whilst I cannot see exactly what happens with him, he isn't on your side, that's for sure." There was a second pause again, hearing her cussing at Twinkles, her Russian Blue, over the phone, muttering something about a scratch on her leg.

"Stella, focus. You say this is important. Back to Connor."

I can sense her pause to think, which only leads me to wonder what if this won't work. Then Stella says, "All you need to do is find a way to get to her."

"How do you know where she is? I know you're

good at locating people, or creatures for that part, but to find an exact location, including the exact time it's happening is extreme."

"Hey! Don't talk shit about my powers. However, yes, you're right. My visions aren't always 'live' but luckily I recognize 6th Street."

A chuckle leaves my chest. Of course, she should know it well, considering that's where we ended up after she envisioned a human boy at the mercy of a demon. Thankfully, the demon was piss weak, barely able to defend himself.

"It also helps that it's in the same apartment building, so the rest of it is up to you following the scent of werewolves. Anyway, I'll text you the address. I believe she does not know of the Prophecy either, so this will be all new to her. I saw the confusion in her eyes. At least you knew what you were turning into. This girl... well, she's not getting your luxury of insight beforehand." It's easy to imagine her saying this, putting one hand on her hip, as she narrows her eyes at me. This was the usual gesture when we had heated conversations. However, with the direction of this conversation, Stella must be keen to get the ball rolling.

Great. More drama creeping its way into my life.

"Okay, thanks, Stella. I'll text you with updates to keep you in the loop. Take care." I hang up, rushing over to the door, aiming at getting a few items before needing to find Connor. What would I tell him? I have yet to figure it out, because I don't want to bother him with the details, rather just bring him his queen. I don't care what he does with her. They can live long, miserable lives, for all I care. My aim is to get out of the house of horrors. To finally live on my own terms.

Besides, Stella contacted me directly, formulating the plan to help me, not to run to Connor blabbing away the whole scheme.

I can bargain my freedom by bringing her to him. He gets his Queen. I happily bow out. This is my chance to get away from the bastard. No doubt Connor will always have me on speed dial. But the crave for freedom from him is the obsession. To cut the strong string that ties us together, leaving the shreds, destroyed beyond repair.

I grin as the plan sinks in. This could be perfect.

Now, I just need to make up a decent lie to Connor, then be the future brother-in-law who saves the damsel—well, technically Queen—in distress.

Hopefully, she won't sink her fangs into me as a thank you, but I guess only time will tell.

****

Back in my room, I chuck the important belongings into my backpack, which brings on the feeling of déjà vu from all those years ago when I did the same thing back in Los Angeles. In no less than five minutes, I'm ready to get out of this hellhole. I just have to see Connor first.

I lock my suite door, then stride over to the dining room, where I know Connor is eating his dinner. The sound of a female's moans vibrate throughout the hallways. I can't say it's sickening to do because I also ate that way at one point, long before realizing I could do it another way without instilling pain.

Even now, I remember clearly how a few decades ago, Stella made an acquaintance with a vampire who was also a doctor working at a small hospital not too far from Santa Monica. After a meeting with the doctor, I resorted to compelling him to supply me with blood bags every fortnight. I can last long without them, but by a fortnight, my strength decreases.

My alternative, which admittedly has been resorted to at times, is to consume the blood from animals. Yes, it's a fucked-up situation, but after everything I've been through, I guess it's easy to view my life as fucked up. I do what is needed in order not to hurt innocent humans. From my perspective, drinking from blood bags or even animals is far better than chomping on an innocent human's neck. There may have been little love in my life, but at least I know I'm not a blood-thirsty monster like Connor.

Standing outside the door, I look at the intercom, which is all twenty-first century-like, but the connection between us is well before technology took over our lives. Instead, I exhale, then make a knock that vibrates loud enough for him to hear it. Although, he probably knows I'm here anyway, with his heightened hearing. Our own scents are similar too, which is presumably due to us sharing a womb.

"You're interrupting my dinner time. Now, brother, that's just impolite manners. You should know better," Connor says, his tone airy yet controlled. But I don't miss the hint of annoyance. If he were in a bad mood, he would snap at me. At least I came at the time he was in, let's just say, a favorable frame of mind. I've seen worse.

My lips thin at his comment. Cocky son of a bitch.

I grab hold of the handle and, with caution, push open the door. As I enter the room, I do my best not to focus on the perky redhead sitting on his lap with a glazed look in her eyes and that all too familiar scene of blood trickling down her neck.

Connor, however, looks pleased as he slowly wipes his mouth with a napkin. He then whispers to his dinner, who smiles and stands up, swaying a little as she moves. Once she leaves the room, Connor slowly turns to me. Raising an eyebrow, he swipes his tongue over the sharp fangs, then plants a satisfied grin. I don't bother reacting because it'll do me no good, so I just raise my eyebrow back at him.

I can see Connor's pleased expression flailing as he rolls his eyes. "Well, I'm waiting for you to speak."

Contain the eye roll, Zachary. Don't do something to piss him off.

Maintaining eye contact whilst maintaining a casual expression, I say, "Sorry, but this is important. I need to head off tonight. There is a new hospital that's opening soon, and I want to discuss the supply of blood for me."

I pause, noticing the glare in his eyes as I mentioned an alternative way to eat. He dislikes this alternative lifestyle, encouraging the animalistic method of drinking from humans instead. As long as it's discreet, which means all the 'fun' happens inside the house. Hide the puncture wounds, keep the yummy good-looking ones alive. The difficult ones, well, they don't return home. I always negated the idea, but he says it 'keeps up with tradition.' Such an idiot.

I choose then to continue, trying not to take his glare to heart.

"But knowing your feelings toward that, I will focus on getting it supplied just for me. Call me selfish, but if I can organize this, then I won't worry about my contact getting queries on the amount of blood bags available. I don't know how long it will take me, but I doubt I'll be away for too long."

Feeling confident about the white lie, I put on a poker face, hoping he would buy it.

Connor simply rolls his eyes, flicking his hands in a gesture that shows he doesn't care.

"Fine. Off you go. There isn't much of a reason for you to be around anymore. I'll call on you if needed. You're dismissed."

As I do everything in my power not to yell or attempt at wrangling him, I simply nod and hurry out of the room, glad that Connor bought the lie.

If he didn't and saw right through me, well then there'll be hell to pay. I know that from experience.

The flashback soars through me as I recall how he locked me in the 'guest' room. The room where he kept his 'snacks' playing with them at his leisure. He would leave once someone fully sated him, with his cleaners doing the dirty work in the end. For me, 1990 was a dark time because Connor became more delirious with power. The decades following 1924 were just a building point and then it turned into an explosion of power. An obsession with controlling everyone around him.

The vision sears through me, nauseating me on the way.

"Stop it! I did nothing wrong, Connor. You can't force me to drink from an innocent woman," I yell as I struggle to get out of his tight grip on my arm. "She's eighteen, so you—" I crash into a door. The loud bang echoes.

Connor's angry gaze is directly on me, his fangs baring out with the signature red pupils. "She was part of the banquet! Do you not see how rude it is to refuse to drink from someone I choose? I don't give a shit if you think she is too young or too innocent—they are our supply of food. I prefer them to vampires, and with the role I have, I can very well choose whoever I want to sate my hunger from!"

Another push and my back slams against the wood again. I try to straighten up, forcing myself to stand against him, but I freeze the moment he gets closer. The fear I have for my life penetrates through me as if this could be the moment that he finally breaks my neck. Or rips out my jugular. Both methods he prefers. His hand reaches for the doorknob instead, then hastily opens the door, pushing me further inside. I steady myself then take a glance around the room, only to realize where I am.

I raise my hands. "No, no, please, Connor. Don't make me do this!" But all I get in return is a sly gleam. He is enjoying the punishment that will destroy a piece of my grip on humanity. He turns and leaves, the oak door left ajar. I know what happens now. I've seen it done before.

Moving further inside, I find a corner in the room and guard myself there, as if it's my own naughty corner. A moment later, the door opens, revealing the young woman I refused to drink from appears. There is no compulsion spell for her to willingly come. She fully comprehends that her life is going to end at the hands of a vampire. Standing there, shivering, with her face wet from tears. I smell the salt on her skin. The door closes, but I still hear Connor's demand.

"You will eat the dinner I provide. Now she is awake to know her suffering, and it's all your fault.

Perhaps next time, remember that at least when I have banquets, it's all dealt with compulsion."And then he slams the door shut. The elephant in the room is heavy as we both look at each. I wouldn't admit it to Connor, but the truth is that I honestly am hungry. Now here she is, standing before the grim reaper.

Was this all my fault? Did I not have a say in at least who I wanted to drink from?

Her voice finally comes out of her mouth, the tone croaky as she says, "P-please don't kill me."

I can't look at her pained eyes anymore, finally giving in to the monster inside. After that night, I learned my lesson. Connor's cleaning crew came as I left the room, ready to cleanse the room from blood and the hacked flesh. The bastard had the audacity to stand there, leaning against the wall. His arms crossed against his chest with a daring smile.

To top the entire experience off, he hands me a serviette as I walk past him, doing my best from ripping his neck. "You've got a little blood on your chin." Connor points to his chin with a matter-of-fact expression. I growl, snatch the serviette then storm off. He must have pleasure in knowing how much I hated surrendering to the monster. Killing someone I was so against, someone that I simply wanted to protect from myself. Instead, it backfired.

Snapping back from the reverie, I'm left feeling distraught, reminding me what Connor is capable of. No one stands against him. Not even when it comes to drinking from a young, innocent teenager. What infuriates me still is that Connor knew that bloodlust could go haywire if not controlled, especially if the vampire hadn't eaten in a while.

I'm just another pawn on his chessboard. I guess this was his way of saying 'checkmate'.

****

Not too long afterward, I set my focus on the text message from Stella, needing to get to the Queen as soon as possible. There is no room for doubting Stella's visions, which rarely fail her. Rushing down the steps, I make my way to my new charcoal Tesla. I may not care much for the high life like Connor, but I certainly appreciate cars, and a Tesla has been on my wishlist for a while.

The drive is smooth, easy to find too, thanks to the address Stella sent. Aside from that, I know the streets of Santa Monica well enough. As the streets pass me by, I glance at the time, noticing that it's well into the evening.

Finally, I see the building and slow down until I find a place to park a street away. I switch off the car and get out of it quietly, ready to stalk within the shadows toward her apartment.

The stench of wet dog hangs heavy in the air, making it easy to trail. I rush my way up the stairs to her door, only to find it open. Slowly, I sniff the room as I enter, catching the heavy scent of blood. My fangs elongate as the blood calls to me, and I follow my gut, knowing it would lead me to the future Queen.

Chapter Six

IVY, EARLIER THAT DAY

Santa Monica, 2021

"Happy twenty-first birthday!" My parents sing loudly in unison, making me have to lower the volume on the steering wheel.

"Thanks, Mom and Dad! You didn't have to call from Australia. We could have just Skyped tonight. It's expensive, guys, but I love hearing your voices. I still can't believe you moved, though. It's been a year but feels like yesterday when we were saying our goodbyes," I say as I catch a tear that falls, but it's not a sad tear, it's a happy one. After all, they have always dreamed of going caravanning around Australia after watching a documentary about the Australian Outback.

Mom laughs. "Oh, enough, Ivy, you're going to make me tear up again. We called because we couldn't wait to hear your voice. Our only daughter has become a full adult and can officially drink. You know, Ivy, in Australia, you've already been an adult for three years," she gushes over the phone. "Also, the place we're staying in doesn't have good internet coverage, so Skyping won't really work tonight, but we are heading toward Darwin tomorrow, so maybe then?"

"Oh, okay. That's a shame, but fair enough. I'm planning on heading down to the studio and then catch up with Damien later today, so tomorrow we can have heaps more time to talk!"

"Sounds like a solid plan. Love you too. We'll speak tomorrow." They make a few kissing sounds, and then hang up, leaving the car in silence.

I lean back and let out a sigh. "Twenty-one." I'm still in disbelief at how quickly time flew by.

A beeping sound breaks my thoughts, and I quickly grab my cell to switch off the blaring sound of my alarm clock app. When I notice the time, my mouth widens, the grin I hold is the same I get every time I switch it off.

"And now for the fun part." I already feel giddy about starting my first class of the day. My holiday program was Damien's great idea, already filling up with the kiddies.

A smile stretches across my mouth as I look up at the quaint studio, awaiting my presence. This is by far my biggest accomplishment. It has been three years since that argument with my parents and I ended up persevering, choosing to chase my dream of studying dance. Now, I'm also teaching it.

I pull off my sunglasses and hop out of the car, excited to see what the day brings.

****

I love dancing but teaching young girls and boys, full of enthusiasm, excited to learn the moves, ignites my soul. Seeing my passion in the eyes of the young generation brings joy.

The classes finished with girls and boys laughing, having the option to do free-form dancing. I love ending my sessions that way. Not sure about how the parents feel, paying for structure and precision, but hey, they're kids who naturally need to run around enjoying life.

I walk over to my car, sorting through the trunk, sifting through makeup, tutus, and ballet shoes galore. I look under my leotards to find what I'm looking for.

"Aha! There you are." I reach for a small box with a card attached to it.

It was Damien's birthday last week, but he was on a family trip so wasn't able to celebrate with me. That doesn't mean he won't get a present, though. I've been looking at the guitar pick for his twenty-first, finally finding the perfect one.

Suddenly, I feel vibrations coming from my cardigan's pocket. Swiftly grabbing the cell, I glance at the name. I grin and tap the green button.

"Well, speak of the devil."

Damien's tone is indifferent as he says, "Hi, Ivy, we just returned from the trip."

"That's great! I can't wait to see you and celebrate your birthday. I have a present for you too!" A smile spreads across my face. "Can't wait to see your reaction."

"Uh, yeah, thanks," he starts quietly, which surprises me, as there is zero happiness in his tone. Then again, for the past year, he has been acting odd. Very unlike him. I still get confused by his change of behavior. He isn't excited about the same things anymore, doesn't even show an interest in playing on the pier as he once did. I thought the pick would be a nudge to get him back into the groove.

Why is he acting so strange? "Are you all right, Damien?"

There's a pause, followed by a sigh. "I need to talk

to you, Ivy. It's important."

My smile disappears quickly, a frown replacing it. "Umm, okay, now is fine. I just fini—"

"No, it has to be in person. The sooner the better before anything happens," he affirms, surprising me with the seriousness in his tone.

My lips thin at his response, but my brows furrow once I process his words. "Wait, what will happen?" Yet all I hear is silence on the other line, making me lose my patience. "Damien, you barely spoke to me all week. Now you're giving me cryptic sentences. Please, what's going on with you?"

All I hear in response is an exhale. "I'll see you in an hour. Go home." His tone reflects his indifference, the deep voice barely sounding like him.

Before I have another snappy retort ready, the line cuts out.

I grumble and shove the cell back into my cardigan pocket. I take my frustrations out on the boot, slamming it a little too hard. Grabbing my keys, I sink into the soft seat, secure the belt, turn on the ignition, and then I speed off toward my apartment.

****

The drive home doesn't take long, considering I found my apartment ideally close to the studio. But as soon as I step out of the car, a dizzy spell washes over me. My hold on the bag loosens, making it drop to the floor as I lean my hands against the window, inhaling several deep breaths.

"Woah, that came out of nowhere," I mutter, rubbing my eyes. Picking up my bag, I turn toward the staircase. "Argh! When will they fix this damn lift! I am over this whole staircase business." Rolling my eyes, I drag my body up the stairs, notably slower than usual.

By the time I get to my door, which feels like a lifetime today, as soon as the key unlocks, I gasp. My body tenses and a rush of cold sensation washes over me, cascading my body. I rush inside in case another dizzy spell hits, letting the door slam behind me. Dropping my bag near the kitchen, my body settles on the couch.

Before I can take another deep breath, the pain returns but doubles in intensity. It's inscrutable, with everything hurting now—my face, mouth, body, all erupting in aches. As I sit on the couch, feeling like I'm soon going to become an icicle, I look down at my hands. "What the hell?" I inspect them, no longer sun-kissed, but pale.

My long hair, which I had taken out of its braid when I was sitting inside my car, falls over my shoulder like a curtain. I then notice another change. I grab a lock that stands out and thread it through my fingers, gasping at the sight. "What's going on?" What used to be chestnut brown hair is now much, much darker. It's a deep shade of black, reminding me of the color of ink, flowing in lustrous, thicker waves unlike before.

I stand to run to the mirror for a closer look, but tumble, hitting my knees on the carpet with my hands flying to my mouth. "Argh! Mother f—", I shriek. Suddenly, I taste something odd, like a metallic taste inside my mouth. Blood.

My hands fly to my mouth, with one index finger swiping the top of my tongue. I look back at it, still reeling in pain, tears flooding down my face. Indeed, blood covers my finger, and an icy chill courses through me. At that moment, something sharp junctures through my gums.

Tears pour like a river as I reach for my gums, hitting something solid. Longer, sharper than a standard tooth. "Ow, ow, ow!"

There's a knock on the door just as I begin to check the other side of my mouth. "Damien?" I ask loudly.

"Yeah, it's me. Can I come in?"

I note the concern in his voice. Tears pour out as I sob. "Yes, please, please, come in!"

Damien opens the door. Seeing my state of distress, he rushes over to me quickly and kneels beside me. "Shit, Ivy, are you all right?"

"I don't understand… I was fine, then suddenly when I came home, my body started aching so badly. And then, then…" More sobs hitch my breath as I touch my jaw. "What the actual hell is going on?" Frustration and confusion ooze out of me.

Suddenly, Damien leans over, grasps my chin, and inspects my mouth. By the look on his face, I know something serious is happening to me.

"Fangs!" he whispers. Then his eyes snap to mine, and I notice the tension as he gets up. "Ivy, did you know? Have you been hiding this secret from me all this time?"

"Know what? I hid nothing from you. You should know that. How can you accuse…" I can't find the words to finish the sentence because a widening sensation in my gums begins. Suddenly, just as before, a wave of ice shoots through my body again. The pain, unbearable, and I let loose a roar. "Please call the ambulance, Damien. I can't bear this pain."

Damien bends down beside me, but just when I

think he is going to help me up and take care of me, he grabs my chin, tilting my head toward him. His eyes crinkle with a flash of sadness, but it disappears quickly. His gaze locks on mine, then with pure conviction, he says, "Vampire... You're turning into a vampire, Ivy!"

Freeing my chin from his grasp, I slowly rise from the patch of carpet I've now stained with drops of blood from my mouth. "What are you talking about? There are no such things as vampires. You know I don't believe in all that mythical nonsense." There's a moment of silence, which infuriates me because this isn't how Damien acts, ever! "Things like vampires and other fantastical creatures are found in books and...films." I finish, irritation clearly present.

Suddenly, I hear a low growl and turn to stare into Damien's eyes, to see if he also heard the growl. But the sight of bright yellow pupils immobilizes me.

My mouth drops open. "D-Damien... Your eyes," I stutter.

All he does is cross his arms and cocks his head. "Ivy, your fangs."

My voice hitches, but I try to push through a pang sensation of light-headedness again. My fingertips are back to my gums, sliding them over the sharp fangs that are now openly protruding through my pink gums.

"What the hell is happening? This...can't be real." I mumble, still in disbelief. Then I look at Damien's eyes. My eyebrows furrow as I turn my head and take a double glance at his face. "Your eyes... What's going on? Are you a vampire too?"

A mixture of a laugh and growl vibrates through his chest. It almost sounds as if he's offended. This doesn't impress me at all. Here I am in need of emotional support, scared and trying very hard to not show my anxiety rising inside. Yet, he just stands there nonchalantly, throwing off freaky vibes.

My anger rises, like a kettle almost at boiling point. But I do my best to push it back.

"Damien, what is happening here? I'm so frickin' confused... You're looking down at me with yellow eyes...and acting like it's totally normal! I have fangs!"

Damien's lips thin, and I see in his eyes that he's planning an explanation. Or at least, I hope that's what it is. Finally, he sighs and says, "There is so much that you don't know, even I didn't know it until recently. Ivy, I can't be here with you now that you're a vampire. Talking to you, explaining things...helping you is the last thing I should be doing. If it were another vampire, I would rip your head off and then stake you just for dramatic effect." He finishes with a scowl.

The harshness of his words hit me like a slap across my face.

"Wh-who are you? This is not the way you would ever treat me. After all these years—" I pause and shake my head— "you look at me in disgust and speak to me like I'm an enemy. We're best friends, not strangers."

I gather some courage in this confusing and fragile state, daring a few cautious steps toward him until I can rest my hand on his arm. Damien flinches at the touch and grabs my wrist.

"If only you knew how much *is* at stake now that you've turned."

I have no idea what to say. His hand wraps around my wrist. The moment I glance down at it, he lets go, like he can't stand my touch. Tears of betrayal fall despite trying to wipe them away profusely, wishing this was all a dream.

"Please, don't distance yourself away from me, Damien. I refuse to believe that after over a decade of friendship, you can turn around and flick me aside."

The cool exterior lasts for a snippet longer, but then I see a flash of pain in his eyes. For a second, a spark of hope lights up, but before it ignites, he's back to being this stranger. The pain strikes again and I fall to my knees. Looking up at him, attempting to stay strong, I say, "If this is how you are when I am in such pain and in my most vulnerable state, then you have shown your true colors. I'll call an ambulance on my own."

Damien just stands there, showing no sign of moving. "And what will you tell them when they see you? How will you explain your fangs?" He laughs. "That will be fun."

Under the callousness, that comment is all it takes to realize that I am, in fact, totally screwed. My head throbs, feeling so foolish thinking that I can just tell him to leave and have a paramedic give me painkillers. To offer to take me to the hospital is a human biological response. Clearly, I'm no longer normal—it would raise lots of questions.

The throbbing increases and that metallic taste sours my tastebuds again. The aches vibrating through my body, coming back with a final stab, with my eyes shuttering. All I can do is listen to Damien's voice. "You can't run from this, Ivy."

"Why?"A whimper croaks out from my lips. Pain elevates.

"Because of the Prophecy. Don't you know anything?" He sighs. Lifting his head toward the door, he suddenly goes ramrod straight. "I've got to go. I've been here too long, and you're the person I should kill, not discussing the future with. Don't call me or try to contact me anymore." Damien walks toward the door but pauses before he leaves. Finally, I hear a whisper of words that I've been waiting to hear from him.

"Happy Birthday, by the way." Then Damien steps out of the apartment.

The slam of the door is the last thing I hear as my eyelids struggle to stay open.

And then, not a minute longer, my eyes close and my body surrenders the fight into a dark abyss.

Chapter Seven

ZACHARY, ALMOST TOO LATE

The potency of blood is overpowering, but what I hear is worse.

Muffled screams. I can hear the struggle without needing to see it.

My mind is whirling, hoping to make it in time before they hurt her. The door is ajar, not making it too obvious someone has broken into a resident's apartment, but it's a stupid move to still have it open. Sloppiness. I note the relics drawn above her door frame, an ancient spell to shut out the noise. That's why no one came to help her when she screamed.

I can hear the struggle vibrate through her shrieks. "Get off me, I don't even know what your talki—"

"Shut up!" a woman snaps, and that's what urges me to quickly push the door wider. I make my presence known. Unfortunately, the view makes me regret not arriving earlier.

Two large werewolves occupy most of the space in the lounge room. A female of what seems to be a wolf in human form, straddling a young woman. Her hand is wrapped around the neck and her legs caught between the sharp, threatening jaws, ready to gnaw them apart.

Suddenly, their eyes snap open, and the werewolves look at me. And just as with any threatening situation I find myself in, my fangs shoot out in defense. "Get. Off. Her. Before I tear you apart!"

The female snarls at me, and barks directives at the two wolves by her side. "Boys, end the bloodsucker!" Then she suddenly extracts sharp claws and slashes them against the woman's face. She screams, the sound strained by the clasp of the hand around her neck.

Before I have a chance to speak, the mutts are charging toward me. My threatening reactions kick in and, in a flash, I do what the vampire council forced me to learn as part of their training. They believed that if I were a resident and assisting Connor; I needed to know how to defend him.

I run with unnatural speed between the two werewolves, and with a mighty force, I land a punch at both of their throats simultaneously. It's quick and powerful and certainly unexpected on their end. I caught them off guard, which was the plan.

They growl at me, saliva pooling in their jaws as if they were ready to play with dinner. The difference is that I won't be their dinner. Anger colors their eyes, the yellow shining bright as the glaring sun. They slowly retreat and bark at the female who is slashing at the young woman beneath her.

She stops and lets go.

"What do you mean, not worth it? If I tell you to kill him, you fucking kill him." Her eyes glow yellow in anger toward the wolves, who now stand apart from their leader.

"If you want to live, I suggest you step away and retreat. And quickly. Otherwise, your clan will find themselves missing three from their pack." My threat hits them as they snap their jaws and roar back in retaliation.

Quick as a flash, I'm in a fight position, fully expecting them to pounce, but instead, they retract and bark at their leader. Something is going on and any other day, I'd find it intriguing to see what will happen next, but that's not part of my mission.

The woman's eyes widen in surprise to see them retreat instead of retaliating. Using this distraction as an opportune moment, in an instant, I have the female in my grasp. A snarl rises from my throat and with my elongated fangs, I take one quick bite into her jugular, piercing it hard enough to make her scream and see the fear seep through her eyes. I retract the fangs, proving to them how much I am not playing around, and throw her against the wall.

The force of the crash against the wall is loud, and I can hear glass from the picture frames break as they fall onto the floorboards.

She clutches her neck as the blood flows like a river, but she is strong, and attempts to get back away. I step forward, quickly glancing at the reflection of the two mutts in the mirror, which thankfully didn't break, working in my favor. I can see they hadn't made a move. Not even to help guard her when she hit the wall.

Their fear reeks, and the monster in me enjoys the power over them. I take a calculative glance at the woman lying on the floor, covered in blood, and shaking as she watches the surrounding scenario. But it must have taken longer than I expected. Before my eyes, the female gets on all fours and transforms into a large white wolf. She may have been injured in human form but isn't as affected when she turns into her wolf form, which derails my plans.

Her growl is sharp and vibrates throughout the apartment. Ready to pounce on me, she begins her attack, but I'm too quick and powerful, slamming my foot against her head before I swiftly land behind her. She stumbles and howls, blood dripping from the forceful hit.

The other two howl in unison before they bounce out of the apartment without even looking back at their leader. She snaps her head and barks, clearly pissed off at these downright pathetic pussies.

I smirk as I watch her flounder because she's now not in the best position to fight me again. She appears dizzy from the hit, and her white fur is now matted with the pooling liquid, reminding me of blood staining soft snow. The scent is potent but far from delicious. In fact, it's disgusting.

The wolf looks down at the woman, who is now going in and out of consciousness. I can see she is contemplating finishing the task at hand. I run toward the young woman and pick her up, laying her gently across my extended arms and snarl at the wolf as I bring her closer to me, in a protective stance.

"Try it. See if you leave this place in one piece."

She growls one last time before bounding out of the apartment, following her fellow mutts.

I know I should have killed her, and this might kick me in the ass because I know they will try again, but I haven't killed in many decades. I no longer have it in me. It only leaves me with despair.

My eyes peruse the petite body in my arms as I hold her close to my chest. Lying still as though dead, I take in her scent and come to terms with how she is no longer alive. Her heart isn't beating. It's now still, just as mine is. The transformation has taken place. I don't know when she started transforming, or how it happened, but I know one thing. She is too delicate and innocent to go through this. My transition came at twenty-one, but it's hard to see it on a young woman who no longer has a chance at a full life ahead of her.

I move toward the bathroom and tenderly place her in the bathtub. Finding a small cloth, I rinse it with water and then run the taps. Getting her clean from the blood that has stained her body seems like a good start.

When the water is finally lukewarm, I fill the tub up to where it just passes her mid-arms. She stirs at the movement and twitches her nose slightly when I place the cloth on her cheek where the claws sliced through. They are healing ever so slowly, as expected for a newly turned vampire.

I push aside her matted fringe, standing up, taking a proper look at the woman lying in the bloodied bathtub. She has a petite frame yet a lithe figure and skin so alluring, fair and flawless. Reminding me of a porcelain doll. My gaze then falls to her closed puffy eyelids. Her tear-stained face makes my emotions, for an unknown reason, rise. I see pain. Someone whose spirit had given up the fight. If only she knew there was no fighting this fucked up world.

I squat beside the bathtub, looking at her in what feels like fascination, and lower my voice. "What's your name, sweet?" The term of endearment surprises me, though. I've never said that to anyone. Past and present.

Suddenly, two watery amber eyes open. She blinks a few times, no doubt her vision adjusting to the light. Then her sight falls onto me. Her pupils widen and she shrieks, making the water splash.

My reaction is quick, and I stand up, retreating backward so she gets no more frightened than she already is. I lift both hands in defense. "Don't worry… as much as it may sound cliché, but I truly don't mean you any harm. I'm here to help you."

Great. Really fucking smooth, Zach.

Despite my reassurance, she continues to look confused and worried. It's so clear in her eyes. She's exquisite and expressive. For a moment there, as we look at each other, I swear I feel lightheaded.

"W-who are you? What happened to…" Her words are husky and slow, but she doesn't finish the sentence when she glances toward the door. It's enough for me to understand her question.

Before I explain everything, I want to give her space rather than lurch over her like a creep, so I walk over to the sink and lean against it. My hand reaches the back of my neck and rubs it, formulating my words into a suitable response. "My name is Zachary. Not sure if you remember what happened earlier, but… I'm also a vampire, just like you. And for the mutts, well, they were an inconvenient distraction, but I took care of them. Do you remember what happened before I came?"

She doesn't respond, instead nods her head, and then glances down at the water in the bathtub. "Uh, why am I…?" She swishes her hand through the water, furrowing her eyebrows as though trying to remember what happened.

I point to the drenched towel with heavenly scented blood stains. "There was blood all over you after the attack and with you being passed out, I thought it would be a good idea to get you cleaned up. And then you woke up." I try to be as nonchalant as possible, but truthfully, I don't like the situation I'm in. I didn't want to fight off mutts and to be so vicious, or to see a beautiful woman drenched in blood for something she probably didn't even know she was a part of. And fearful of me. Speaking of fear, I consider how overwhelmed my senses were when I first smelled her blood. It's never happened before, and that's what surprises me.

I look at her and notice how uncomfortable she seems in the bathtub. Her clothes are soaked right through, the cream tank top clinging to her skin, giving me a splendid view of breasts hidden behind a purple lacy bra. The water saturates her shorts, making them adhere to her sexy curves. I do my best not to ogle her any longer before she notices. I clear my throat. "Do you want to get out? You won't catch a cold from the temperature of the water, but it might still be uncomfortable..."

She nods and slowly lifts herself. She doesn't even try to suppress a wince, which I find cute. I forgot how emotive humans are. But she isn't human anymore. She just hasn't lived long enough to realize that immortality interferes with emotions.

As I shuffle over to the towel rack, grabbing a soft, clean one, I hand it over to her. "What's your name?"

"Ivy Litt," she responds curtly, which is understandable. I don't doubt the transformation and attack overwhelmed her. A tiny part of me is expecting the shoe to drop and her to freak out at me, too. Ivy accepts the towel and wraps it around her body, but then quickly drops it. "Oww! Gosh, no, not again!" Ivy screams as she grabs hold of her jaw. Then her stomach. "Could you please hel—" But she doesn't finish her sentence, shrieking as she slips.

Rushing over, I catch her in time. The feel of her soft skin makes goose pimples rise, and I almost regret touching her. Almost.

Gently, I lift Ivy up and cradle her soft body, shuddering from the effects of the pain. "I got you, hold on." She may have passed the transformation part, but her body still needs to adjust. I found it the toughest part of the whole bloody ordeal.

I only need to take a few steps forward until I stand at her bedroom door, wide open and inviting. Underneath the wooden door frame, the room can only be defined as the brightest bedroom I'd ever seen, and admittedly, I've been in many women's bedrooms over the years.

Pastels of blue and yellow hues splash across the walls, and flows into her linen. It's so gentle and...happy.

As softly as possible, I sit her down on the mattress.

"Thanks." Her voice is soft however, her demeanor changes suddenly when Ivy seems to realize the situation, because she props herself up and swiftly shuffles away from me.

The space between us is large. We might as well be on opposite ends of the room instead of the bed.

Fuck, this is not going as I planned. It's awkward and I feel like a moron.

She shudders and goose pimples rise on her pale skin, amongst the faint freckles that sprinkle over her arms and shoulders.

I grab a folded blanket off the bed and hand it over to her. "Here you go." I stay still, trying to give her space, even though what I really want to do is wrap it around her and get close enough to…

Concentrate. Get a hold of yourself, Zach!

I interrupt my internal monologue when Ivy takes the blanket and drapes it around her shoulders. Her mouth turns into a frown, and I hear the huskiness in her voice. "I feel so weak, and my stomach feels like someone is tying knots inside of me. And a blinding headache and now my gums ache so much."

As she mentions the pain, I notice tears dribble down her cheeks. I stand up from the mattress and turn to face her with the hopes to calm her nerves, but looking down at her feels wrong, so I sit on my haunches, trying to be calm and understand this whole situation is new territory for her. Then, as if it's second nature, I bring my thumbs to her face and wipe the tears away. Maybe it was because my mother declined my help as she lay in pain, or possibly my sudden attraction to Ivy. I can't figure out why I did that. It was an intimate gesture, and we don't even know each other, not to mention I'm going to be her future brother-in-law.

Just as I did earlier, I lower my voice again. "I know it's quite a lot to deal with." This prompts her to lift those two captivating amber orbs back at me.

Ivy nods silently, looking as if she is trying to keep her emotions at bay. Adjusting the blanket, she tightens it and says, "How did you know where I live? You appeared out of thin air."

I rake my fingers through my hair as I contemplate what to say without overwhelming her. The questions are valid, but it's not the time to explain everything to her yet.

I give her a slight nod and straighten to my full height, shoving my hands into my pockets. "It's a long story and honestly, we have more important things to talk about. Look, why don't you get out of those wet clothes and change, then meet me out in the living room? We can talk more, but it's best to be in a better mindset... and comfortable, before I divulge more information." I pause and then thin my lips before I say, "Let's just put it this way—you're up for an interesting ride."

Ivy lets out a chortle and rubs her temples. "I've been on a ride since my body became possessed with pain, aching and bleeding gums, even pricked my frickin' finger on a sharp fang, and to put the cherry on top, giant wolves attacked me. Somewhere in between, I also passed out. So, I doubt whatever you tell me will blow my mind."

My thinned lips turn into a curve.

Well then, aren't you in for a surprise.

Chapter Eight

IVY

Once Zachary leaves the room, I collapse onto the bed. Exhausted, I lean back into the quilt and stare at the ceiling.

What's happening to me?

I hear a shuffle outside and revisit the entire conversation. He's a vampire, and a strong one too, with the way he had to fight off three werewolves. The attack was vicious and unexpected, but he saved me without even knowing a thing about me. Or why I was being attacked.

The thought of the vindictive-looking woman and two large dogs entering my apartment and pouncing on me forces bile to rise in the back of my throat. My body was not only shattering on the inside but on the outside, too. My screams did nothing to gain attention. Not even one neighbor came by to check on me.

Last time I make desserts on Halloween for the whole fucking building!

The feeling of heavy tights is a reminder that I'm wearing soaking wet clothes and the reason Zachary left my room so I could change.

Zachary...the stranger who looks empathetic, and nothing close to the other creatures that preyed on me. His demeanor is the opposite. It's a sad thought, though, because this is the reaction, the care, that I hoped to get from Damien.

That sad thought whirlwinds into a tornado of anger and I ball my hands, hitting the mattress, sputtering curses at him.

No, no, don't let the betrayal get to you!

The hissy fit doesn't last long as the image of hypnotizing blue eyes, pale skin that closely matches mine, and a body of hotness fills my mind. My nose remembers his scent, the whiff of soap and citrus. An odd mix for a man, especially one who deems himself as a vampire.

The thoughts of Zachary ease my irritation, and I rise from the bed and walk over to the closet. I rummage through it until I find my favorite sportswear. Despite the worn-out look, they still get away by looking good as new. Plus, it's so comfortable and compliments my physique. I dress, slip on my Skechers, and walk over to the mirror, situated on top of my overflowing chest of drawers, thanks to the lack of space in my room. One glance at my reflection and I am sent into a state of panic. I look like Snow White, minus the short black hair and dress. Okay, technically, just my skin is freakish, like the cartoon character. My fingers run through my hair, dark and smooth, opposite to what it looked like this morning. I need to get used to this color and texture. My eyes remind me of honey, a lighter shade than the darker hues of brown I'm used to seeing in the mirror.

I'm an image of someone else, apart from the usual pert nose and full lips, which I can't stand. I look different. Strange. Supernatural.

Right, I'm supposedly a vampire now. How the hell

can this have happened in one day? My life…shit, my parents!

My pale hands cover my face as I quietly sob, everything slowly sinking, realizing my whole life has come crashing into a pile of rubble. The shitty part is that I have absolutely no choice in it. I can't even pick up the shattered pieces of my life. I have no family here in the States, at the moment, or my amazing class of students anymore. Not even dancing will fix this. I'm not human anymore, and I'm not delusional enough to expect I can return to my ordinary life.

I wipe the tears with my sleeve, even though my true self would use a tissue. I just don't give a damn at this moment. A fucking vampire, a creature…who lives for blood! Blood. My face pales more, if that's even possible, as I look at myself and realize that a standard drink of water won't even suffice me anymore. That I will have to rely on drinking blood, and only blood. *Or maybe I can avoid it altogether? Hmm, yes, I can try fighting it.*

There is more shuffling outside, and it reminds me that technically, a stranger is still inside my apartment. The brooding, wistful, yet devilishly good-looking vampire who saved me, without even knowing who I am. It still baffles me, but something about him allures me. Makes me curious and brings out a desire to learn more about him.

The thought surprises me and I shake my head at the silliness. *Pfft, forget it. He may be hot, but he is a vampire, and I won't mix with those creatures. Even if I am now one of them.*

Chapter Nine

ZACHARY

Whilst waiting for Ivy to change, I message Stella
with an update, and then take in the surrounding room.

To say they damaged the entire living room is an
understatement; a lamp on the floor shattered to
smithereens, the coffee table knocked over, and shards
of glass all over the ground. As I pace around the room,
taking in the mess, something hard underneath my foot
grabs my attention. I move it aside and notice a lock
that I assume had once been attached to the door. I
shake my head at the mess we left. Typical. Those
brutes are ruthless, but then again, so are vampires.

Midway between my thoughts on the werewolves
and this trashed room, Ivy steps out from the bedroom.
Her skin is alabaster yet reflective, like the moon, a
beautiful contrast against her tight navy tank top and
leggings. And fuck, she wears it well—the material
shaping all her perfect curves. Her beauty and allure
enchant me. Unfortunately, she must have noticed me
staring longer than I meant to because by the time our
eyes lock, she places a hand on her hip and eyebrows
arch up.

Whoops.

Slightly embarrassed and annoyed with myself that
she caught me ogling, I quickly muster a "Sorry," only

to receive a remark back.

"Sure, you are."

I smile inwardly, hiding the amusement at her quip by dismissing her comment, and instead, I walk over to the couch to sit. Politely, I gesture for her to sit beside me. Of course, my presence seems to still be unwelcomed because Ivy continues to keep her distance, shaking her head and stands in place, examining me.

Then she glances toward the living room door and says, "The only reason I'm not calling the police is because you saved me. You didn't attack me even though you're a... m-monster, like those wolves."

I look over to the door and notice it half open, so I quickly stride over and close it to give us privacy, especially now that the runes have disappeared. Along with the mutts.

I shake my head and turn around, shoving both hands into my pocket. "Werewolves, actually. You must have been out of it to witness the shape-shifting. And by the way, you point the finger at me for being a monster, yet we have the same fangs. We went through the same pain..."

Wait until you feel the same disgust in yourself. The shame of being a creature who lives on blood.

Ivy's frown depicts her dislike for my comment, her shoulder sagging in defeat. Knowing that she needs support, I walk over to her, warily though, as the last thing I want is for her to distance herself. I stop in front of her. "Thanks for not calling the police and making a big scene. This is a messy situation." I gesture around the room, making her acknowledge for the first time the state of her apartment. But she says nothing, just nods. I can see she's taking everything in, but my frustration with her stubbornness is blooming. I take out my right hand from the pocket and slowly rub the back of my neck, a habit that I still haven't been able to throw since I was human. "Ivy, I'm here to help you. Just accept it."

Her eyes, again reminding me of an amber stone, or one could even say honey, stare back, examining me. At first, it looks like she is trying to intimidate me, but the attempt falters and I notice her gaze sweeps downward, lingering a little longer and then back up to my face. Her expression is obvious to read, and I sense the bloom of interest developing. The oddest thing is that I'm starting to like it. It feels rather good knowing that she ogles me, too. Except, she is much better to look at, dressed like that.

I wonder if she is wary of me because of my appearance. Black jeans, a black shirt to match the gloomy cloud that hovers above my head. The one that's been attached to me for many years, 1924, to be specific. My hair is now shorter than it used to be, with a slight buzz cut on the sides. Some gel their hair, some comb it. I ruffle it and start my day. The top covers the small tattoo of an eternity knot with a sword slashing through it. It matches my view on being an immortal. It sucks and is worse when you find out that you're born to turn into a vampire. Eternity is a long time and, in my perspective, nothing great comes out of it. Not without someone to care for or love, or vice versa. I learned the hard way.

Sitting on the couch, I shift back to make myself comfortable. If she's going to just stand there, I'll just sit here until she accepts the situation. However, this stalemate doesn't last long when her gaze breaks as she rubs her cheek, pressing down against the gum. I can already sense her discomfort and the pain that will come soon enough.

My gaze flicks to her mouth for a moment, and then I cock my head and say, "You'll eventually get used to the sensation. It's painful at first, but then it comes to a point where you don't even feel an ache when they shoot through."

Ivy closes her eyes, likely hoping that it would come around sooner than later and whispers, "Eventually..."

Finally, she makes a step toward the couch and sits beside me. Not too close, though, keeping a certain distance from me.

I swivel to face her, and then move on to the next step—the discussion. "So, like I said earlier, my name is Zachary. A friend of mine has the ability to see into the future. She asked me to come and help you during your transition. Sensed you are still adjusting. She also mentioned that you were being attacked." I pause and then add, "I'm no knight in shining armor, but I am here to help you with your transition."

I notice how Ivy takes a deep breath at my explanation, and even without knowing her inner thoughts, it gives me the impression she is processing everything. Before she speaks, I stall her by putting my hands up, a silent 'hear me out'. "There's more. I know about the pain..." Ivy raises an eyebrow but stays quiet. "Yeah, I know the feeling. But I also know the next feeling. The...hunger."

Licking her pink, pouty lips, she slightly nods her head. "I'm hungry. But I refuse to do it. I've been shutting out the thoughts, so don't even get me started on drinking."

Ivy confirms it in such a stern tone, but the battle between giving in to her desires contradicts her facial expression. It was evident she was the type of person who wore her emotions, which is something that needs to change. Vampires are excellent at reading people's emotions, which means if someone has a bad poker face, they are in trouble.

I rub the back of my neck, the frustration already affecting the muscles in my neck. "Look, I understand what you're going through, but regardless of how you feel about consuming blood, if you don't, you will continue feeling weak. Along with weakness comes more pain and discomfort."

Ivy smacks her lips together, the fight inside visible in her facial reaction. I can't let her go through more pain and weakness—it can lead to death, even for a vampire. That's a fundamental similarity between humans and vampires; both can die from starvation.

Still, she keeps her lips pursed and shakes her head. I take a deep breath and slowly exhale, trying to calm my frustration. How am I supposed to help her if she doesn't want to help herself? As gorgeous as she is, sitting in front of me was someone with a death wish.

"Ivy, you seriously need to drink some blood, and I won't leave until you do. I'm here to help and guide you through the transformation and after-effects, and then bring you to the Vampire King." I don't want to elaborate further, preferably avoiding the part where that vampire is my brother. "Look, I know you don't want to drink blood, and I get it, I do. The transition is a pain. As I said, I'm quite aware of the feeling, but at least you have someone here who can help. You can't run from it. Your survival is too important for us, vampires." I say, the words flying out of my mouth.

Her eyes widen at my ramble, catching her off guard. I continue, needing to get this all into her head because, well, she is just too much of a walking wet dream to die from starvation. "When you first turn, you need blood to regenerate, which will lead you to gain strength and get a grasp of what is happening to your body. Now, I don't have any blood bags with me, so you will need to use my blood. It's not something I do—drinking from other vampires, so don't get the impression we feed on each other. Some do, some stay away from the act."

It's considered taboo and I also find it odd in general. What's the point of drinking from humans? But almost a century of why's and how's still never gave me an answer.

Ivy's two mesmerizing eyes blink back at me, clearly surprised that vampires can drink from their own species. But then the surprise disappears, and her stubbornness reappears as she crosses her arms against her chest and says, "I already told you I won't drink blood. No freaking way am I going to drink what runs through a person's veins. Frankly, I don't care if I die again, because I'd rather that than become a monster!" Uncrossing her arms, she flings them up and cries out in exasperation. "Before Damien and the werewolves minced out words like Prophecy and a future Queen Vampire, which I still don't understand what that all means, my life was simple and fun. I danced, played instruments, sang, and taught dance. My preference for movies and books is all romance and comedy, not dark paranormal fantasy... I still feel like I need to pinch myself." Ivy takes a pause and rubs her temples before she swings her gaze back to mine. "Look, Zachary, thanks, but no thanks. Maybe you should leave. Go tell the vampire to move on and find some other woman to fill in the shoes of a future blood-sucking monster."

"Sorry, but I can't take that as an answer. You don't seem to understand how important you are for the Prophecy. Ivy, you can change the way vampires live, the way they drink and prey on innocents," I say, admonishing her ignorance, even if she is still in the dark when it comes to the Prophecy. Well, technically, I made it seem like she has a positive part in this.

Pursing her lips, she crosses one leg over the other, a defiant stance again. Who is this beautiful, stubborn woman? My eyes gaze along the length of her legs, hidden under those sexy leggings. It's becoming hard to focus when she looks so delicious and innocent at the same time. My thoughts quickly disperse, however, by the sound of hunger. Yes, our stomachs rumble. Sounds ridiculous, right? But if we have blood thumping to our dicks, have sex, orgasm and cum, then surely our stomachs can still gurgle when hungry. It sounds bizarre, but I got to admit, I like it because it reminds me of the familiar way I used to feel when I was human.

I lean forward, look at her and do the best serious expression I can. "You need to eat, Ivy. I know it and you know it. I want to help you, not make this worse for you."

"What about you? Where do you stand with killing innocents for dinner?" Ivy says as she raises an eyebrow and looks directly at me, peering into my soul.

Clearing my throat, my eyes gaze away from her.

"Uh, well… I don't like to bite humans, or other vampires, or vice versa. Usually prefer to save that for more…intimate settings." An instinct in me rises and, for some unexplainable reason, I really want to know what she tastes like. Would it be bland like the ones I have tasted before, or decadent and smooth?

I snap out of my reverie and continue, "Anyway, I prefer to drink from blood bags, which are supplied from a hospital or…sometimes animals." Before she can say anything regarding animals, I thrust my hands up in a 'wait, there's more' gesture again. I feel that's all I do to stop her from jumping to conclusions and not hearing me out. "But only in dire situations, though. It's when I get desperate."

This seems to calm her a little. I expect more questions, so I give her some time to process, but instead, she bursts out in laughter. And yes, the 'covering a hand over her mouth trying to calm herself down' laugh. Once it finally ends, she shakes her head with a grin planted on her face. "Intimate setting? You can say I prefer it during sex. It won't offend me."

Fuck. I wish I could swallow my words and that the ground would eat me up. She literally laughed in my face. Don't millennials understand manners and chivalry?

This was my attempt at not scaring her away with cussing and talking about sex with vampires. I do everything I can not to give her my rebuttal and an eye roll.

The sarcasm in my tone doesn't go unnoticed as I say, "I tell you I drink from blood bags and animals and 'intimate settings' is all you think about?"

"I guess I want to ignore that disgusting

explanation. Then again, at least it's not seducing and killing innocent people by robbing them of their life," Ivy says back.

I scoff at her comment. "Can't say that I seduce innocent people and drink their blood, but I can say that I prefer innocents to walk away unharmed. Even vampires. Let's just say I like to keep to myself and be far away from drama as much as possible. Now, back to drinking."

Her demeanor changes, and the apprehension grows in her eyes. I notice a common habitual trait as she stands in place, twirling her hair around one finger, frowning. Ivy shakes her head and whispers, "I-I, umm, have an unpleasant history with blood. It gives me the heebie-jeebies." I notice she gives a slight rub of her arm. Soon after, she sighs and shakes her head, shoulders slouching—a vision of defeat. "Ah crap, I really didn't want to drink blood. I won't lie, though. I feel pretty weak and trying hard to keep up with everything. Hell, my feet feel like jelly, and gums are now aching again. When I felt the pain the first time today, it was so painful, it brought me to tears, and frankly, that's the last thing I want you to witness... It's not the prettiest thing to see." Her gaze flits to my face again, then my body, and then back up. Is she shy about looking weak in front of me?

With a quick nod, though, understanding what she is feeling, I move closer. If anything, I want to reassure her. Console her. It's the weirdest thing. "The gums, they ache because you're hungry and can smell my blood. It's a vampire thing, which you will eventually become accustomed to. Right now, your entire body is calling for blood, and it doesn't discriminate about whose blood it is. We may not have a thumping heart, or not breathe, even though we still sigh and exhale, but blood still flows through our veins as does in a human. It's confusing, and fuck, even a contradiction to simple biology and vampirism altogether, but there is no explanation except it is what it is. I doubt a vampire sat down and learned why we still have human mannerisms and some biological functions, so I don't know much about the matter." I feel it's time for a pause. She needs to get a handle on her new situation, and I'm getting tired from this lesson.

I sigh and continue, "Regardless, it's a necessity for you. From what I have heard in the past, no self-inflicting damage has been successful. Even suicide won't work, and trust me, it's not a pretty sight to see a friend try to off themselves. As a science experiment." I finish the words gruffly because I am still furious at my friend's stupidity. He did end up dying, though, just in battle.

Ivy's eyes widen a little, followed by a cute bite on her bottom lip. "And you went through this too? Is this normal when humans turn into vampires?"

I give a quick nod, not particularly liking the question, yet I answer it the best way I can. "Yes, and no. When a human gets bitten, they need to be buried immediately, if not shortly after the attack. When they finally die, they rise and, well, they're then part of the walking dead group. For me, it was different. Trust me, I'll always remember the excruciating pain and how it leaves you with unanswered questions as to why it's happening—the 'why me?' part took the longest to overcome. The difference is that when I turned, I was literally alone in the dark, hiding away inside a small room at a brothel that I managed to sneak into. Whilst everyone downstairs drank and laughed, I was lying on the floor screaming from the pain. It felt like my body was on fire, an inferno blazing through my insides, even though I was conscious enough to know it wasn't."

I pause, my mind going back to that day. She can't see what I do, but Ivy needs to know what happened after I turned. "Another difference is that when I finally gave in to my hunger, there wasn't much of a brothel left... So, I'd say, me being here with you is a blessing because if it weren't for me, you'd either die from starvation or find an innocent person for dinner, and I have a good feeling that the latter is not very appealing to you."

My message must have registered because of the hard swallow she makes and the watery eyes making their appearance again. *Fuck. This is not going well.*

Arguing isn't productive, and I really need to find out more about her. More so, I also needed to get in touch with Stella and find out the next step in her 'save the vampire' plan. My thoughts are quickly interrupted as Ivy fires questions in my direction.

"What happens after? I drink your blood, feel better and... what then? Damien left me in the dark and disappeared as soon as he realized I was going through the transformation. Once he saw my fangs, everything about him changed. He left me. My best friend...just left me. I didn't do that to him when his eyes glowed yellow!"

Damien? Hold on. Who the fuck is Damien?

I want to ask her, but Ivy is in her own world, pacing back and forth, anger seeping out. I can sense it.

Coming from someone who didn't grow up with many friends as a human, and felt the safest without vampire friends, I can't say I know what Ivy is going through. But the way she's speaking, trying to form sentences as she processes what her friend did at that moment, he found out she was different, really must feel like a stab in the back. She is so expressive. It's like a roller-coaster ride every time I look at her. And then suddenly, like a delayed reaction, the words 'eyes glowed yellow' make me rise from the couch, realizing it's something that humans don't do.

"Glowed? And what happened after that? Did he attack you?"

I know I'm hurling away questions, but the overprotective feeling washes over me, and I can't seem to help myself.

Ivy shakes her head though and sighs, twirling a loose strand of her hair. "No, he didn't, but mentioned he couldn't be close to me—that I'm his enemy and his priority would be to kill me. Then he walked out of the apartment with only 'Happy Birthday' being his last words to me. I can still hear the door vibrate as it banged, as if he slammed the door on my heart."

I nod but stay silent, my thoughts trying to process what she said. *Werewolf. Her best friend is a werewolf. Shit, that's not good. But why is killing Ivy his priority? I need to speak with Stella. Possibly she would know.*

Attempting to explain the truth is going to be hard, but I need to be blunt about it. Just like I am with everything else, or at least most of the time. I cross my arms against my chest and roll my eyes. "Ivy, please stop moving. You need to know the truth."

Ivy halts midway and turns toward me, the amber

orbs full of curiosity. She nods and I know it's my queue to start.

"Look, I'm going to be honest with you. This Damien character you're acquainted with is a werewolf. But aside from that, what's most concerning, though, is that he knows more about you than he should, which isn't good news."

The gasp that comes from her is loud, shocked at my revelation. "Werewolf? Is that because I told you his eyes glowed yellow? How can you simply accuse him of being a monster based on that?"

I nod. "Yes, I assume that because only werewolves have yellow eyes. All paranormal creatures have specific eye colors. It's the best way to recognize the type of creature you're dealing with. Around humans, they can change to the usual brown, blue, green and gray, but as soon as they are around other paranormal creatures, their eyes morph into their original colors. Although, I must note that those colors are only when their emotions are in a heightened state, which is usually when they're pissed."

Her head tilts slightly, curiosity gone and replaced with confusion. "Wow, eye color represents different factions? But wait, our eyes aren't red."

My lips twitch at her questions, but I suppress a chuckle. It's so hard not to laugh because everything she asks is valid, but the innocence behind it is humorous. I am not that old of a vampire, but have been around long enough to have seen a big part of the paranormal world, so it's not common for me to explain these things to others. Especially as the ones I deal with already know the various factions we have.

When she rubs her temples, undoubtedly

processing that vampires aren't the only creatures that walk on land. I know it's time to give her a quick rundown. The rest of the creatures are just as twisted and dark as Connor. Ivy needs to know this in advance. Fairies aren't cute. Wolves are dangerous and menacing. Witches don't fly on broomsticks, instead will do whatever they can to use magic to their advantage. And demons.... well, that's a whole other story of evil. She literally just became part of this dark world, swarming with deadly creatures.

"Yes, the color of their eyes determines the factions. As I mentioned earlier, it's based on our heightened state. If you hunger to kill your prey, your eyes will also turn red."

Her deep exhale is loud and shaky, which leads me to realize she's probably freaking out. *Maybe I pushed it with the in-depth details? Shit.*

"So, Damien is a werewolf? All this time...and never told me?"

Shrugging my shoulders, I give her my opinion. "Would you if you were in his position? It's difficult to say, 'Hey buddy, I'm a vampire, but don't worry, I won't drink your blood. Pinkie promise'."

A small giggle slips from her mouth, and despite the topic, I find myself grinning. "Hey, I know it might seem like total shit how Damien left you, but at the end of the day, he is an enemy, and he wants you eliminated. Now, I don't know much about him and why he knows you're connected to the Prophecy, but I'll speak to my friend and see if she knows anything about it."

Ivy gives me a slight nod and then swipes her tongue against her gums, reminding me she needs to drink.

And that's when a light bulb moment comes to me. Compulsion!

I grin at Ivy, proud of my concept of having her drink whilst she is compelled. She looks back at me like I'm nuts, but I don't care. It's perfect. "I thought of a way for you to drink without having to do it consciously. I can compel you to do it. You will be in a haze and have no control over it, to the point you may not even know what you're doing."

Her mouth opens slightly, those amber eyes in shock. "Are you frickin nuts? That's ridiculous!"

I lean toward her and shake my head. "No, it's the only way I can think of where you get to drink and not have to think about it. You won't realize a thing, and that's the beauty of the idea. You don't want to drink, you have a fear of blood, yet you must consume it to live. When you are under a compulsion spell, you have no choice but to do it, yet at the same time, you aren't technically conscious of your actions."

I wait for a rebuttal, but Ivy simply nods, even if she wears a frown. She may not be happy, but this is the only method I can think of. Rolling up my sleeve, not caring if it gets crinkled or bloodied, I make the move, openly making myself her prey. "You'll need to get closer and control your nerves," I say, gesturing for her to move nearer and close the distance between us.

Ivy stares at me, her glance moving from my eyes, down to my wrist, and then back to me. I give her some time to decide, but the way she stares at my wrist gives me the inkling she knows exactly what she wants. And I'm right because she gradually walks over and sits beside me, surprising me when she scoots closer. For a moment, I think she's finally relaxing, but it flutters away as I sense the nerves flowing off her like a river.

"Relax, Ivy. It's like a form of hypnotism. I'm going to talk very slowly and calmly. Just focus on me, that's all you need to do," I whisper, focusing on calming her down rather than giving a reason for her anxiety levels to increase. "Look deep into my eyes. Don't say a word. Don't think."

Ivy nods and turns to look at me. Her amber orbs aim directly at mine.

My lips move slowly as I enunciate the words, infusing them in her mind. "Ivy. Forget the fear of blood. Take my wrist. Puncture the skin. Drink from the vein. Stop when I tell you to."

As I lift my arm and move my wrist closer to her mouth, it registers we were sitting very close to each other. In a way, it actually feels intimate. This was why I didn't enjoy doing it like this. It feels better when both were in a more sexual mood, not shy if it led to foreplay and sex. What happens if I get turned on whilst she drinks? That'll be awkward for her and really embarrassing for me.

The thoughts quickly vanish as I feel the sudden grab of my wrist and sharpness sinking into my skin.

Chapter Ten

ZACHARY

Yep, it happened, just as I hoped it wouldn't, but apparently, my cock is too excited to have an attractive woman bite into my skin and drink from me.

Rather than gently biting the artery, she was feral, clinging herself to my arm. With her mouth on my wrist, she pulled on the vein so hard I had to clench my fists and try not to hiss from the pain. Not that I'm a pussy with pain thresholds. Nevertheless, it fucking hurt like hell.

The way Ivy drank from me was different from what I assumed it would be, though. I expected I would have to guide her and she would put up a fight. Guess she must have been starving because it felt like I was the dinner, and for the first time in a very long time, I felt pain when being fed from and, as expected, it was indeed messy. There wasn't just blood on my sleeve, but it stained my jeans as well. In some fucked up way, I like it. Or at least the monster in me did.

She stops drinking and coolly lets go of my wrist, just as I expected her to, as part of the compulsion.

Ivy snaps back to reality and shrieks. "Crap, I'm so sorry, Zachary!" When she notices all the blood on my wrist, along with two deep punctures, her eyes well up with tears. More so, the realization that her hands and mouth are now smothered with red liquid, some still dripping off her chin. To a human, it would disgust them, but for a vampire, we are already comfortable with these sights. Blood is our choice of food. It is just the method of consuming it that differs from one another.

I don't blame her for being spooked. An innocent person would react the same way. Speaking of being spooked, I am also, but for a very different reason. I squeeze my eyes shut as I feel the tightening in my jeans. Luckily, Ivy became too distracted with drinking to notice how hard I was for her when she sucked on my wrist. It felt erotic and painful all at once, like freaky BDSM with fangs.

Ivy takes hold of my wrist and shakes her head. Her eyebrows scrunch as she peruses the area she bit. The puncture wounds are still slightly visible but will soon heal completely, as it always does with vampires of my age.

I cover her hand, giving her a gentle pat, and say, "They'll heal shortly. If it were you though, it would take much longer."

Ivy simply nods and says, "Gosh, we're both a mess." Getting up, she walks over to the tissue box that had fallen on the floor and starts cleaning up the bloody mess. Passing a few over to me, I accept them and do the same, but know that it's highly likely my clothes will stain. Ivy must notice my apprehension as I rub the tissues against my collar and begins to apologize again for her behavior. I wave her off like it isn't a big deal, but that's a lie because some part of me liked it and that worries me. Before, I cared little about the Prophecy and how it will end with Connor being with a mate. But now…

Now, though, seeing Ivy, my image of Connor's happy ending has changed. I look at her and see light. She is beautiful, more attractive than I thought she'd be, and remarkably considerate. I mean, Ivy even became apologetic about drinking from me, which adds to her kindness. There was no running from me, but instead, she dealt with this situation strategically.

I pull in a deep breath and exhale, needing to wrap up my disappointment in a box and burn it because nothing would change this scenario. I'm just a mishap, not the King that has every vampire kissing his freaking boots. I wonder if Ivy would like him. She doesn't seem like a person who will enjoy being around a cocky bastard like him… she is too gentle? Innocent. Connor will ruin her. I know it will happen, but it isn't my place to say anything. It's all the Prophecy shenanigans that I have no place in.

When I return from my bitter thoughts, I glance at my cell phone, and coincidentally, it rings. I tap the green button. "Hey, Stella, thanks for getting back to me. So, what's next on the agenda? I gave her my blood to strengthen her and explained a few things to Ivy about—"

"Find out more about the werewolves. This is bad news, Zach. She needs to get to Connor so they can fulfill the Prophecy, but now, because of the wolves, it'd be a good idea to teach her how to fight and protect herself. Just in case. Remember, we want your freedom."

Fuck. Really? Fighting?

This is not what I planned on doing—I was just going to play all nice, then get her to come along with me to see Connor. Now I need to play teacher? Hopefully, she won't need to fight. I don't see the need to do anything more than just take her home. Home to Connor, that is.

The thoughts make me bitter, but I hold my tongue because I don't know how Stella would react to me being unhappy with her vision. She doesn't like me challenging her when it comes to the visions and the decisions based on them. Something about hurting her feelings, for doubting her third eye.

Before I can respond, Ivy comes up behind me. The hairs on the back of my neck stick up in excitement with her presence so close. Her clean and floral scent accentuates the air, as well as the hint of my blood on her lips.

My thoughts fluctuate from lustful to borderline creepy, so I shove them away, returning to the conversation at hand. I straighten my posture and clear my throat. "I doubt there will be anymore clashing with them after what I did to the three earlier today. But sure, I'll work on that. Please send me any updates if you get any further visions. I don't particularly want to walk around in circles. I'll talk to you later. Thanks again, Stella." I hang up, shoving it back into my pocket, and turn. Ivy's back down on the couch, patiently waiting. She must have walked away to give me privacy on the phone. Probably processing everything. I shake my head slightly removing traces of lust from my mind and decide to check out the rest of her apartment. At least it will give us both space and time to deal with our thoughts.

Wandering around the apartment, I notice little things about her place, like how neat and clean the kitchen is, despite the catastrophe her living room is in. Clearly, destroying the kitchen wasn't on the wolves' agenda. My gaze flicks to the cute pictures sitting atop the wall unit. In the middle, a few kids, which I believe to be her students, surround Ivy. The image exudes happiness, them all smiling sweetly as they pose in their tutus. My gaze falls upon a frame on the wall with what seems to be a senior year graduation photo, captured outside where she's throwing her cap in the air. My gaze falls at a bunch of flowers on the floor, sans the vase, which is now smashed. It doesn't take long to realize that if the mess was cleaned up, this apartment would be full of warmth. Peace. Being a vampire, or any creature at least, is not peaceful, happy, or safe. It's a bloody and miserable way of life. How is Ivy going to survive this world? I don't know the answer to that.

"Is everything all right?" Ivy asks as she stands there, looking at me with a quizzical expression. Her face and hands are now clean, but her top is a little messed up. Unfortunately, my gaze lands on her breasts a little longer than necessary. I shake my head and run my fingers through my hair.

I lean against the kitchen bench top and rub the back of my neck. "Well, that depends on what you consider being 'all right'… My friend, the seer I mentioned earlier, said that I need to bring you to the Vampire King, which leads me to the Prophecy discussion. Knowing how you don't particularly want to be a vampire, unfortunately, it ties you into this world. And I doubt you'll see this as *all right*."

I look at her, waiting to see a reaction, noticing her pouty lips now thinned. But she surprises me with a quick nod, walks over, and leans against the kitchen bench right beside me. My body tenses as Ivy stands close, with no hesitation, unlike before. At least she looks better, noticeably stronger. Her onyx strands look smooth and glossy, like what I assume most women dream of having. But mostly it's her eyes that draw me in. They are bolder, even more mesmerising than before. Hell, even her lips turn a luscious, darker rouge.

Ivy lets out a deep sigh then turns around, placing her palms against the bench top as she looks at me. "Look, whatever is happening to me, or will happen to me in the future, I'll have to deal with it. I'm cleaner now, even understand a few things about being a vampire, and know that being with you will be the safer option. Not that I can't guarantee that I won't fall into an ocean of tears. Please don't be one of those people that walk on eggshells around me and treat me so apprehensively. I hate that. So, spill."

Well, if that isn't direct, I don't know what is. It's refreshing too, directly to the point. The need to know more about her life before she transitioned is now becoming more intriguing.

Maybe her view changed because I explained things without sugar coating it? Perhaps that made her understand there was no running from being a vampire, that she needs to learn how to deal with it. I'm not sure, but so far, things are going well. I don't want to ask questions that will make her retreat into her shell.

"Okay. It is said that the Prophecy is an ancient vision of the future where one day, a young man will turn into a vampire, then the same situation happens with a young woman too. The twist is they are born from human parents." I then go on to explain how, in this vision, they unite to become King and Queen of the

Vampiric Kingdom." As I finish, her expression shows confusion, so I give her a chance to ask a question. Like she knows what I'm thinking, Ivy goes ahead to question me.

"So, he is my...destiny? I'm twenty-one years old. Marriage is not on my mind right now. Besides, I always imagined falling in love first before marrying." She pauses, furrows her eyebrows, and says, "How will we know we're meant for each other? Is there a connection that ties us together? This is confusing on so many levels."

I run my fingers through my hair yet again, and shrug. Whether it's fortunate or not, even over the decades, Connor nor the Vampire Council elaborated on the Prophecy. So even I'm swimming at the deep end. "Umm... well, I don't know for sure. Maybe older vampires who have heard of the Prophecy would be more knowledgeable on the topic than me." *Bullshit your way through this, Zachary. She doesn't even understand the concept of the Prophecy. She'll believe anything at this point.*

I look at Ivy and give her a light smile. "I would presume that you feel a connection of some sort. Like a spark and know immediately that he is the one you are destined to be with."

Ivy seems tense at hearing this but says, "Okay, I guess... What else were you going to say? Sorry for interrupting earlier."

"No worries. To be honest, it's quite brave to ask questions. I don't know how most other people would deal with this... Anyway, I was going to say that the outcome of both uniting is positive, in a manner of speaking. From what I've heard over the years, they will change laws for a better, safer, and equal place in the world where we live, among other paranormal creatures and humans. My role here is to strengthen you mentally, physically and help guide you to the Vampire King to begin creating a better world for us. The end," I finish with a lopsided smile, with the hopes she wouldn't run from me. But despite the smile, the uneasy look on her face remains. Clearly, Ivy's not elated by what she has just heard. Why would she be?

I just became a massive asshole by feeding her that ridiculous lie. Why would anyone believe there could be a better world for vampires? I guess, like innocence, naivety is bliss too.

Ivy's eyes widen. Yeah, the expression on her face depicts her reaction to what I had to say. Her apprehension and fear visible as she studies me, not even bothering to hide her feelings. Before she would try to say something, my hands move to her shoulders, attempting to calm her nerves.

"Let's move on from that to werewolves. We can't be going around in circles, Ivy. It's understandable that you're scared, but…think about it—you can make my life as a vampire better. I hate the way others hurt humans, even other creatures." That's not a lie because it actually reflects my feelings about the way vampires treat innocent humans. "Now, let's talk about this Damien person and the werewolves. You need to explain what the hell happened in here," I say, waving a hand toward the mess on the living room floor.

It takes a few minutes before Ivy opens her mouth and begins. At first, her expression was peaceful when she spoke of her time being a dancer and singer with a future career as a dance teacher. And how it all changed one night.

"Damien…was my partner in crime. We've known each other for years. He was amazing on the guitar, and I used to dance to his tunes. I can also sing a little, so we used to muck around on the Pier dancing and singing to his music. It was silly, and probably nothing amazing, yet we had a great time."

Her grin is beautiful, happiness floating in waves as she recalls her past. But then I hear a hitch in her voice when she mentions Damien again. An urge to want to know if they were in a relationship, or if she had feelings for him, suddenly appears. But I keep my mouth shut and let her speak.

"I called him, instead of my parents, complaining of being sick. At first, I thought it was the flu, but the pain moving to my gums and body felt like it was on fire, worse than any cold or flu I've ever experienced. Anyway, he came over and was…different. It's hard to explain, but he was distant and grumpy. Then, with one look at me, noticing me rub my gums, he suddenly became wary of me. Like he wasn't sure he should be there. He was my best friend. I didn't get it at the time, though being under the impression he was just being a douche, but then h-he…" Ivy pauses, trying to calm herself down before adding more. "He grabbed hold of my chin and forced my mouth open. When he noticed my fangs growing, he abruptly let go of me. He mentioned the Prophecy then swore, like he was angry at me!" Ivy exasperates, anger seeping in her expression.

I purse my lips, feeling her anger, understanding how it hurts to be kicked to the ground by someone you rely on.

"What happened after he saw your fangs?"

"Well, long story short, he told me I'm turning into a vampire. I found it ridiculous and told him he was crazy, that paranormal creatures were fictional characters from books. There is nothing realistic about them. But then he lowered his eyes for a few minutes and then lifted his head and... his eyes glowed like two yellow orbs. And, well, after that, it all went downhill. He mentioned that we're considered enemies. Don't know why or how he changed, though. I thought we could talk about it first, then he could teach me more about this world..." She pauses, then lowers her voice. "I just thought someone I trusted would be there for me. Hell, I was crying in pain, yet he just stood there, looking at me like 'Oh, that's a shame.'"

Ivy's expression says it all. Yes, she has words to describe how it all went down, but sometimes you could see how one feels looking at their facial expression. The betrayal.

"I know the feeling, Ivy. Trust me. Not that I'm going to talk about it, but you aren't alone in a world where the people you trusted or depended on thrust you back into the gutter and make you feel as if you don't matter. I don't know this Damien person and how much he knows about you, but just in case, I'm going to get more information on him."

I pick up my phone and text Stella.

—Hey, do you know anything about a werewolf called Damien? He was friends with Ivy. Thanks, Z—

Almost immediately, she responds.

—Yes! Not good. He is the Prince of the Gray Clan. I have heard talks of him being taught how to lead the clan. His father is sick, and he is next in line. Get her to Connor with no wolfy attacks.—

Now it makes sense. Looks like he freaked when he saw Ivy, his newest enemy, and bolted.

"Fuck," flies out of my mouth. This whole situation is getting more dramatic as the hours go by. In fact, it's been a couple of hours since I found Ivy and things are not getting any easier for her.

Ivy places her slender hand on my shoulder and squeezes it as she asks, "What? Did you find out more about Damien?"

I take a few seconds to comprehend how nice and warm it was to have Ivy touch my shoulder, despite the stained shirt as a layer between us. I nod and muster out an answer, despite wanting to just enjoy her closeness instead. "He is the Prince of a clan of werewolves called the Mighty Gray Clan. Pretty much your enemy. We need to leave and get you safely to the Vampire King. Now, first, get a bag ready with a few belongings, then we can head off."

"Prince!" Ivy gasps.

Just as I mentally prepare for the next step, I remember Stella's comment on having Ivy learn some fighting skills. Or at least get used to her vampire abilities. She seems to have transitioned, but the side effects have yet to all come into effect.

Question is, where am I going to be able to teach her all of this?

"Actually, before we go, there is something that you need to learn."

"Seriously, there is more?" Ivy sounds displeased.

"Along with your transformation, you don't just need to feed. You will have special abilities such as—"

Ivy crosses her arms, interrupting me with a roll of

her eyes. "Yes, I know. Just like in all the books and movies. It's the heightened scent, clarity of your vision, hearing is stronger, and you move really fast."

It's hard to suppress the vibration within my chest as I chuckle. I haven't had a deep laugh like that in a while. Ivy just based her knowledge on books and films. Who is this beautiful millennial? However, her gaze narrows at me, making me suddenly remember that the female species doesn't enjoy being laughed at. It usually ends up awkward and with the way her eyes are throwing daggers toward me, it's clear that finding her amusing isn't a good idea.

Sinking back a little, I hold up my hands in an effort t to save myself from a potential outburst. "I didn't mean to laugh at you, Ivy. It's just that you base everything off someone else's imagination. You can't assume things because an author wrote it down decades ago, or that it's portrayed in films. I found it a bit unexpected, that's all."

Ivy huffs, hands resting on her waist, cocking her eyebrow and says, "Well, then, please do tell what there is to know, seeing that I am jumping to conclusions."

Trying to form the examples, I pause, realizing she is right for most of them. *Shit.*

Ivy looks at me expecting my explanation and all I can think of is how beautiful her deep amber eyes are, and also how do I tell her everything she said is mainly true without sounding like an idiot for laughing at her in the first place? Her mouth slowly turns into a teasing smile. "Come on, surely you must know all there is to being a vampire."

"Well, you will be faster, and I mean incredibly fast. You'll be able to hear things very clearly and have the ability to sense things from afar. Along with that, the vision will be clearer in the dark an—"

"So, technically everything I just said earlier, just paraphrased?" Ivy's facial expression reads "I win!", which is annoying yet cute at the same time. But this is a pro's game, and I won't let her cruise through this.

"Well, you never mentioned that walking in the sun just gives us all but a slight tingle over the body, and that we can't get burnt or die from the sunlight. Or that not only staking can kill a vampire, but also beheading them. It can even take longer depending on the age of the vampire. Or that we can go into an insane blood lust if we don't learn how to control our hunger and abilities. You're pretty much screwed if you don't know how to protect yourself. You also need to have an understanding of exactly what you are and how you can use your abilities on predators. Remember, just because they consider us monsters, there are others on par with us. There will always be other monsters that look at us as prey." Ivy's mouth widens as she shudders, seeing her attempt at controlling her breathing. "Sorry, sweetheart, but this isn't a game. It isn't a story or film. It's your new reality."

I walk over to her slowly, hoping she gets the picture, but the closer I get, the more apprehensive she is about me. I see in her eyes that she is retreating away into a shell.

As she stands there against the door, unsure of my next move, my hand reaches toward her arm, something I never intended to do. I lower my voice and try to be as gentle as possible. "It's a scary world. I won't lie about it, but you have me here and I want to help you learn how to protect yourself. You'll be fine swee—" I pause at the words because it slipped out the first time, and now almost made its way out again. I clear my throat and try again. "Ivy. You'll be fine. I'm sure of it."

Glancing down at my hand curled around her arm, she quietly says, "Thank you..."

I quickly step back and nonchalantly rest my elbows on the kitchen sink.

Yeah, try not to make it awkward, Zachary.

But it's not like I intend on acting awkward. It's my emotions running wild. My thoughts are blurry, not as rational as usual. Truthfully, I think my intention of simply bringing a mate for my brother has gone out the window.

Chapter Eleven

ZACHARY

The concept of retreating to a place where no one will find us falls into plan. Figuring out the logistics is what I do best and have no room for doubt.

I rub my hands together and say, "Okay, so this is what I am thinking we do. We need to find a place where I can show you some simple moves to use when retaliating in a fight. You'll need to find a way to deal with your new abilities at the same time. If you know even a fraction of self-defense moves, it's better than nothing."

Ivy nods, but then her eyebrows furrow and she says, "Is this really necessary? If I am going to be Queen—gosh, that sounds ridiculous to even say out loud—what reason would there be for me needing to fight? Won't I have some security guards watching over me?"

"I don't know what's expected for your protection, but I presume as you are a target by the wolves, it's just being extra cautious of others who may attack you. Last thing you want is to freeze when you're attacked by a creature, or even a human. Self-defense is important, even if it's a simple hook punch or a kick to the groin."

Ivy nods and then gestures toward the living room. "And where can we do this? My apartment isn't large enough."

"True, and it's not safe here anymore, but I have an idea," I say, before taking my phone out.

****

I scroll my way down to S and click on Stella. Our history as partners in crime goes a long way back, since she appeared on the estate's doorstep in an invisibility cloak. It was the oddest thing, but really fucked with my mind and she found it funny. Although, it was far from that. There was no humor in it—curtains swaying in different directions, the coffee table shaking and rattling. I got a bit worried for my sanity, thinking it was a ghost, so headed straight to my room like a pussy. Just because my fangs protrude from my gums, doesn't mean I enjoy the company of ghosts.

Stella must have followed me, and I remember how I yelled "Who's there?" when the knocking wouldn't stop against my door. Then the doorknob turned, and I shrieked when it burst open.

But in that space, there was nothing. No ghost.

The genuine shock came when the door slammed shut and suddenly Stella appeared in front of me screaming 'Boo!'

Needless to say, my reaction was very un-vampire like as I jumped back. Once I realized what happened, my fangs shot out, a reaction from the monster rising from his shackles. "What in damnation! You scared the devil out of me, Stella!" I didn't miss the irony in that comment though, furious at her.

Instead, her shoulders moved, and her hand covered her heart-shaped lips. Her laughter had rang out. "Oh, Zachary, that was wonderful. I haven't played these sorts of shenanigans in years!" Her smile widened, and then she finally calmed from her childish laughter.

"What in the devil are you doing here? It's been five years since I last saw you," I exclaimed, my fangs still out, but anger in check.

Stella rolled her eyes and retorted. "You can retract those fangs now. Your pride is unmistakable, but I am not an enemy." Then instantly her expression turned apologetic and genuine. She lowered her voice and said, "I presumed you wouldn't be frightened." I didn't need to hear an apology as it was all in her tone.

My fangs retracted back into my gums. Tension no longer rolled off my shoulders, but continued to be flabbergasted at the spoof she played on me. "How did you appear from thin air? What type of jest is this?"

"I couldn't use a horn, so I had to find other means of meeting you. I've been observing you for a while now. In a protective sense, of course," Stella assured me as she scrutinized the room. Dark and foreboding. Like my heart.

But instead of annoyance, or what I assumed my reaction to be, my mouth curved up, and like a goose, I chuckled. "You, watching me? Why? I can protect myself. Or are you here in want of payment for your guidance?"

Stella's hands landed on both sides of her hips and quipped back at me. "Don't be a fool. I wanted to help you and wouldn't ask for anything in return." She paused, and then gave me a smirk. "Well, at least not you. I rather like you, Zachary, and think we could be good friends."

Her confidence was charming, but her words still confused me. Shoving my hands into my pockets, I leaned against the wall and contemplated on being friends with the witch that saved my life from turning into a vicious monster. I would have probably gone to shred apart the town if not for her guidance and care all those years ago.

"Oh, and I see it in my visions. So not to worry, it will happen regardless of what you think. Ponder all you want, but we save innocents in the future. We help each other in times of need, and torment the hell out of one another. Seems rather entertaining, actually." A smile graced her sun-kissed face.

Since that day, I decided that this crazy witch was indeed the only person who cared about me. Enough to spook me out, admit she was following me, and watching me over the years—well, I didn't consider any afterthoughts.

Stella and I became partners in crime from that day on. There were many times when we hated each other, disagreed with each other but we always banded together in the end. She is the closest person to me, and I know she is someone I can rely on.

For this reason, calling her for help is the best—and right—choice.

****

My phone lights up as it rings, and I finally hear her voice. "Is everything alright?" Her worrisome tone surprises me.

"Hey, Stella. Things are, well, I don't know...going with the flow, I guess." I look over at Ivy, and then rub the back of my neck, turning toward the kitchen bench so she wouldn't see my reaction. I don't have a reason to feel concerned or frustrated, but I am. This is getting out of hand, trying to run from werewolves, hiding and then training… it's just not what I expected. I wanted to simply use Ivy as bait and bring her with me to Connor. My straightforward plan. Well, I assumed it would be. The attraction toward Ivy, her captivating eyes, swirling with innocence, and delicate yet bold features, changed my game plan. Realizing this frustrates me, because the last thing I expected was to notice her in this way.

I tap my fingers against the Caesarstone bench top and then continue my spiel. "Anyway, nothing to be worried about. The reason I'm calling is to ask if I could use your studio in Laguna Beach for a couple of nights? I want to prep Ivy before she meets with Co—" I stumble on the name, almost forgetting that Ivy doesn't know much about him except his title. "The Vampire King."

Stella doesn't respond as quickly and eagerly as I expect, which leaves me on edge. I need a place and her investment property is great.

I push for an answer, as time isn't a luxury right now. My tone grows serious as I say, "Stella?"

Over time, we have become protective of each other, and something feels off. I can hear the concern in her tone, and I know she's hiding it. Still, I don't press because I know her well enough to expect her sassy attitude to cover her true feelings. It's been like that for years, and as they say, you can't teach an old dog new tricks.

Her response is a deep sigh and then she says, "Sorry, yes. I'll text you the code to enter."

I can hear a hint of concern, but it evaporates quickly. "Great, thanks for your help, Stell. I can always count on you. Speak tomorrow."

"Glad you can think of me in times of need," she sings and says, "We'll speak tomorrow indeed."

After the call, I shove the cell back into my pocket and turn to Ivy, who is now sitting on the leather couch, her large observant eyes waiting for me to explain my plan. It's so easy to get lost in them. I need to move forward. I can't stand here stagnant as she waits for an explanation.

"Okay, so a bit of a detour from here, but we're heading to one of Stella's properties that she owns. It's a studio and is on Laguna Beach. It should give you some time to adapt and a good hideaway in case the werewolves come back trailing your apartment."

As Ivy runs her petite fingers through her silky waves, a waft of jasmine lingers in the air But the grimace she wears makes me forget her scent for the moment as she says, "My poor apartment... I love this place."

Her frown appears along with her furrowed eyebrows, and it's obvious her thoughts are going in another direction. I know it because that's how I felt at first, too. How life has changed and, in her case, how she will probably never return to her sanctuary. As unfortunate as it is, we don't have time for these thoughts right now.

I rest my hand on her shoulder in what I hope is a reassuring gesture, and say, "Come on. Go grab a bag and pack. We need to head off."

Her mouth lifts, but the smile doesn't reach her eyes. Ivy gives me a couple of nods and then disappears into her room. As her sexy form fades from my vision, I shake my head and take a glance at my phone, which, of course, pings through with an address.

Chapter Twelve

ZACHARY

We've been in the car for barely fifteen minutes into the drive and Ivy shifts in her seat, rubbing her gums. My focus is on the road, but I can see from my peripheral vision her glancing at me and then back to the windscreen.

I have a feeling I know what she's thinking, but rather than dismiss it, I'd like Ivy to think I'm approachable. She needs to be on my side, or at least unafraid of me. Clearing my throat, I glance her way. "Is everything okay?"

Ivy bites down on her lip and shrugs. "Umm, well, my gums are aching again. I'm getting—"

I give a slight nod. "Hungry?" Ivy says nothing, but the hunger is clear in the way she crinkles her eyes and bites down on her lip. I use this moment to continue and explain a couple of things to note. "You don't have to hide it from me. Besides, even if you try, I can still sense it. It's expected for young vampires to feel hunger pangs more often than the older ones. Like me, for example, I can last longer without drinking because of my age."

Ivy imitates my nod. "Okay, so... how do we do this?" I hear the wariness in her voice, but don't understand why until I remember the last time she drank blood, it was mine.

Fuck, and there goes my dick, hard with just the thought of her lips against my neck, sinking her fangs and having me as a snack. Twisted and delicious at the same time.

I'm brought out of my crude images though, quicker than my dick would like when I hear her silky voice say, "Zachary?"

I don't answer immediately because I don't know what to say.

Ivy looks down at her hands as they rest on her legs and quietly says, "Was it that bad that you don't even want to offer again, or speak about it?"

I can hear in her tone that she's disappointed with my silence. But the way I feel about what happened earlier is quite the opposite of what she assumes. And again, I feel bad and want to reassure her.

"No, no, it's just that I hadn't thought about it. I was just thinking about if it's a good idea to drink from me again. Not that you did a poor job, just maybe you should drink a human's blood rather than mine."

She swallows and slightly shakes her head. I don't know how long it will take her to stop avoiding it or find a way to get over her aversion to blood. I am already sensing a stubborn trait in her. It's sweet, but it's an annoying trait at the same time.

Besides, would it be so bad if she drank from me again? And aren't I intrigued to taste her too?

I want to flick away the thought, but my imagination runs wild, and it refuses to leave my mind. Would I get hard again? What would she taste like? My mind conjures the image of me licking the soft skin above her pulse right before biting into it, and that image itself is all I need to leave my concerns far behind. With my increasing arousal and lack of logic because of it, words form, and I thoughtlessly blurt them out. "I think it's a good idea. Besides, I'm getting hungry too. Haven't fed for almost fifteen hours."

Not that it would really matter to a vampire as old as me, so I have no idea where that comment came from.

"Does it hurt?" Ivy asks softly, leaving a sense of curiosity hanging in the air. It seems her interest is genuine, although I wonder if it's because she finds it arousing too.

So, I give her my honest answer. "Yes, at the beginning, but afterward it feels…good. Better, even." The truth in my response makes my dick twitch in excitement. It's like my body is living a life of its own when I'm close to her.

Ivy's eyes are now on mine, and a shy look crosses her face. "Did you feel good when I drank from you?"

Okay, this is going off course. First, it's hunger and now it's curiosity about my feelings on how it felt when she drank from me? As if I'm going to respond with, 'You gave me a boner. Need I say more?' I give her a side look but it's hard to see much as her gaze is down on her lap, fingers rubbing up and down nervously.

"Well, did you?" she asks quietly, the insecurity filling up the car.

My fingers tap the steering wheel in a habit I do whilst driving. "It was painful at the beginning, but I'm used to it, so there is barely any reaction to it now. Anyway, what do all these questions mean? Do you want me to drink from you, too?"

Say yes…

117

"Well, technically, if both of us are hungry and busy avoiding angry werewolves and learning how to fight, don't we need the energy for all that? Having something to eat..." She pauses and points at me. "That's what I am calling it, by the way. Saying 'something to drink' just reminds me of it needing to be blood, which still disgusts me despite having no other option if I want to stay alive. We need sustenance, don't we? Plus, there are no blood bags here so..."

I inwardly smile, happy that she said yes, even if it is indirect.

"Well, I admit, you have a fair point. Didn't expect it, though." I act nonchalant but honestly, on the inside, I'm astonished at her idea. Not only is it rational and a good point, but so unlike what I expected.

I rub my scratchy chin, now covered in scruff. Her answer not only surprises me, but pleases me too.

Instead of deciding against it, she simply justifies why I should drink from her. Like a warning sign flashing, I remember one important fact to point out.

"However, I need to give you a heads up you may feel,"—I pause, not knowing exactly how to explain the likeliness of getting horny— "Well, it can make you feel...aroused."

Ivy bites her plump bottom lip as I say the word 'aroused', and my focus returns to the road. Glancing at her for a second was dangerous, for driving and my brain. Which at the moment isn't functioning well. My peripheral vision is unmistakable and, for a second, I wish it wasn't. Fuck. Those tempting lips. Her amber eyes turn darker, and my eyes fall onto her pink tongue as it darts out to lick her bottom lip.

I suppress a groan and tighten my fist. Never did I

imagine she would be the one getting aroused. I wasn't planning on drinking from her, but now I can't say no. I don't have the strength to say no, nor do I want to.

"I'm hungry! Let's just get this over and done with, then continue on," Ivy blurts.

It appears as if she's trying to settle down with her trepidation. My lips thin as I try not to grin at her reaction. "Okay." I try not to sound too eager, even though that's how I feel. My cock twitches as I glance back at her lips, then quickly back to the street.

Dammit, focus, Zachary!

I gradually steer off the road and find a park that's, luckily for us, secluded. Once I switch off the Tesla with my key card, I turn to Ivy, who is shifting around in her seat, seemingly uncomfortable, or maybe it's eagerness to get it over and done with. I'm not sure, regardless, it needs to be done. "We have to do this discreetly as I parked us in a public area," I say, studying our surroundings. "If we pull this off, we will just look like a couple that's just hooking up. Even better, the windows are tinted. The only change I have done to this baby." I finish by patting the steering wheel, hoping to lighten the mood. "It's difficult to see through them, so it's a bonus for this situation, I guess."

Ivy chuckles and sets her lust-filled orbs on my neck. The tip of her tongue peeps out and wets her bottom lip again, which drives me with an annoying, insane hunger for her. *Is she trying to seduce me or drive me crazy?*

Her eyes finally find mine. "Okay, how do we do this? Do I need to straddle you?"

And there goes my dick again, for fuck's sakes. I thought it had calmed down, but every time this woman looks at me, shows off her pout, or just, in general, does an absentminded movement that looks delicious, it seems to react. Especially a sentence that has 'straddle' in it.

I drape my jacket lower and attempt to tug it over my groin. Anything to hide the fact she made me hard. The power she has over me.

"Ah, yeah, okay," I stumble and before I know it, Ivy is out of her seat, adjusting her legs over me. She does it swiftly, with no hesitation. Almost keen to start.

I grab her waist to steady her as she adjusts herself on top of me as she straddles me. The position is awkward at first, but we get there soon enough, and she is comfortably straddling me.

Well, this certainly wasn't part of the plan.

Doing my best to calm myself, I compel her just as I did before. The sooner the better, before I embarrass myself.

Chapter Thirteen

IVY

Ohmygosh. My body is on fire. When Zachary and I were discussing arousal during feeding, the pulsations in my nether region started a party of thumping. It was like a frickin' nightclub down there.

I'm not the type of person to feel out of control with a guy, but ever since I met Zachary, my thoughts have become muddled, and after that one bite, the concept of drinking from a blood bag is…yuck.

I need someone to get me out of this horny state, but it only gets worse when I notice him adjusting his jacket. I hope I'm driving him crazy with arousal as he is to me.

Oh crap, I'm totally losing my mind over a vampire! What's wrong with me?

His hypnotizing gaze runs over my face and settles on my lips, which I only now realize I've been licking. He doesn't know that whilst he may use compulsion on me, once my tongue tastes his blood, I wake from my subconscious and am completely in tune with what I am doing.

I squirm in my seat, impatient to touch him. His blood is delightful and potent, and I can't wait to have a taste again. His voice penetrates through me and gives me a command that I silently wish for.

"Ivy. Lean your head against my neck. Find the vein, press down, and bite it. Then drink. We're both hungry and have an agenda to follow. Take what you need but retract when I tell you to stop."

My vision goes a little hazy and I have little say about what I do except knowing that I have to drink from Zachary. My face gets closer to his neck, sniffing the blood, and my lips meet the vein that screams for it to be pierced and sucked on.

And I do as it commands.

Chapter Fourteen

ZACHARY

My eyeballs roll back into their sockets with the force of the piercing in my neck, and sheer pleasure courses through me. It's not as sloppy as before, and I feel her hand glide up my neck as if she's ready to catch any blood that drips down. At least that's what I assume. Unless she just enjoys touching me. My body becomes heated, and I find my hands at the back of her neck, pushing her down against me. Ivy moans, the sound vibrating against my neck—without intention, I'm sure. She moves up and down against my crotch and I can guarantee she feels my boner as she unconsciously gyrates me.

The pressure of her drinking is demanding and wonderful, and yet so wrong. I don't know what to do or what to think except enjoy this frenzy.

I remember I told her to finish when I say stop, and it's, unfortunately, time to say it.

"Stop, Ivy."

It feels like Ivy is slightly hesitant, but then stops and retracts her fangs with a slow, sensual lick over the puncture wound. As she lifts her head, I see a very satisfied smile gracing her lips. A very different reaction compared to the last time she drank.

"T-thank you, that was amazing. Delicious!" Ivy

stumbles over her words as she is coming down from the high. Her hands rest on my shoulder. Well, more like grasping, which makes me chuckle. Though I stop once my eyes fall onto her delicate neck. I trace my finger along the nook of it and gently pause at the place I crave to sink my fangs in.

The artery calls for me, commands me to taste the blood. Ivy doesn't have a chance to prepare as I hungrily pierce her skin. She cries at the suddenness of the bite, but soon falls putty against me. Her blood tastes like innocence and sin all rolled into one. I take and take and take. Enjoying the satisfaction that runs through me, giving me strength. And for a change, so much more than that.

The moans that fly out are ever so delicious too, and the way she grinds against me again... *Fuck!*

I indulge to the point where I know it's time to stop. Quickly withdrawing my fangs, I give the puncture holes a light lick.

By now, we are both overwhelmed by the power of the feeding. She's still sitting on top of me as we both pant, trying to calm our breaths. It feels like we just had sex, but without actually going through the motions.

This is the reason why I never enjoy drinking from someone who will not end up in my bed. Because it starts out as rubbing against each other and then, well, I guess if we are going to go with being crass, jumping each other.

Ivy's flushed cheeks contrast against the rest of her pale face. Her fangs fade away back into their hiding place, and the red in her lusting eyes slowly return to its usual amber. I can't help but grin at her, which then just makes her seem bashful.

"Hell, this is awkward," Ivy mumbles as she gets back to her seat and glances at the mirror for any traces of blood. She acts as if she's back to being composed and I wish I could read her thoughts. Is she still turned on? What is this vixen thinking after using me as a snack?

The words fly out before I have the chance to articulate a proper sentence. "Thank you."

Her eyebrows do a cute furrow as she looks at me. "Why are you thanking me?"

A smile forms and I quickly add, "For trusting me, I mean. And doing this even if you don't like it."

Ivy chuckles, offering a shy grin. "You've been helping me from the moment you saw me, so of course I trust you."

I suppress a groan after hearing her because when it comes down to it, once she finds out how wasted her trust is in me, things will certainly be different between us.

Ivy glances toward my crotch and bites her lips. "Thank you, too… and I'm sorry about the…"

My cheeks are on fire, but I hide my true reaction and mumble, "Ah, it's fine. It happens, like I said before."

She nods and clips her seatbelt back into place and miraculously acts back to normal. No hint of or semblance of a woman that was lost to lust, gyrating against me.

Nope, she's gone.

Eventually, Ivy tries to break the awkwardness after the feeding frenzy and says, "So how long do you think it'll take us to get to Laguna Beach?"

My lips purse as I try to estimate the timeframe.

"Around an hour or a little more, give or take. We'll be driving for a while."

Suddenly, Ivy gasps and slaps her legs, startling me at the random reaction. "Oh, we could have stopped by Los Angeles, Zachary! How did I forget about that? If it wasn't for the frickin' blood, I would have remembered to ask if we could do a minor detour."

My hand tightens around the steering wheel, but out of anger this time. Blood boils through me just hearing that city.

Los Angeles. Where it all began.

"No. We wouldn't go there even if you asked, anyway. Forget it." I may sound stern, even rude, but I don't care.

Ivy's eyebrows raise. "Jeez, overreaction much," she mumbles.

I swallow my anger and make a noncommittal shrug. "It'll make this drive longer and we have plans. I don't like when my plans change. It unnerves me." *There, that's a suitable response, and an honest one too.*

Ivy shrugs her shoulders, and leans back. "Fair enough."

There is no chatter afterward, just us turning the radio up, then leaving each other to our thoughts. I know very well mine will be a juxtaposition of the beautiful, innocent Ivy and the image of me handing her over to Connor, dangling her as bait.

****

By the time we pass the sign that shows we are close to Laguna Beach, Ivy groans and says, "Crap, I hate long drives. I need to move my feet." She then attempts a slight stretch. "Plus, the silence is getting boring. Why don't we use this time to get to know more about each other? I mean, I know little about you, and being a vampire as old as you, I'm sure you would have more fascinating things to talk about than I do."

I chuckle, shaking my head, amused by her comment. "You make me feel like an old grandpa when you put it that way," I tease, which earns me a giggle.

"Well, we have lots of time to talk a bit more. I might as well learn a bit more about you. I'm sure you'd rather not listen to someone who hasn't seen the world like you have rattle on."

I know she wants to get to know me, but I don't want to divulge too much information about myself. Still, I need to give her something. "Well, I guess it depends on what you want to know. I've lived long enough to see evil change the world and shape it the way it is now, so…"

Ivy gently puts her hand on my shoulder, then suddenly pokes it, and says, "Looks like someone is a cynic!"

I give her a non-committal shrug and say, "I know it sounds morbid, but you haven't witnessed the events that have happened over the decades. Yeah, good things happened, but so much death and pain… It's what I'm used to, which makes it hard to see the good in the world." A cynic, she calls me. I didn't think about it like that, but I guess in some ways time has changed the ability to see the good in people. "Trust me, Ivy, after seeing what happened during the Great Depression, World War Two, destroying lives of millions of innocent humans, or seeing how people discover diseases they don't have a cure for. I even remember when an acquaintance of mine back in the eighties learned he'd contracted AIDS. When the world became known to the disease, it got ugly, and he had no chance of surviving it in the end. Then, the wars between the supernaturals—all factions—at each other's throats. Remember, they can die too, and die they did. The Vampire King was at his most ruthless time in those years, a sight I will never forget. Oh, and let me not forget the part when I watched my parents slowly die from the Pneumonic Plague."

Realizing my mouth is running off at the depressing things I have seen, I try to pull myself together, reeling in the images ingrained in my brain over the decades. My eyes can't even close to get my thoughts away from the darkness that is my life because I'm driving. I inhale a deep breath and say, "Sorry, it wasn't my intention to go on and on... There just never seemed like there was time to sink into the world's goodness."

I hear silence, which unnerves me. I look ahead as the car is in motion, but steal a side glance toward Ivy. Her eyes are staring ahead, and her hands are laced together against her stomach. Finally, she opens her mouth and fills the car with sound and says, "Wow."

"Wow? After all that, wow is all you got to say?" My tone exasperates my surprise at her comment.

Ivy tilts her head, nodding. "Well, I'm still trying to process everything, and that seems better than 'I'm sorry that you went through all that,' because I consider pity is the last thing you would want to hear."

She's spot on. Call me a cynic, but don't feed me pity. This topic is not starting out the way I thought it would and yet rather than changing the topic, I'm too curious and ask, "Do you pity me, though? Or are you just saying it to make me feel better?"

Ivy sighs and turns toward me, shoving a few loose strands of hair behind her ears. "No, but I don't like how you talk, as if you're the only person who has seen bad things happen and feels angry about it." I open my mouth to retort but come short, leaving her time to continue. "And before you try to argue, let me explain."

"Yes, please do," I say, failing at hiding my gruffness.

"I'm twenty-one years old, Zachary. I left my human life with issues between my parents, stored away in a box because it hurt me at the time. Now I regret any argument or anger I had toward them. I lost my closest friend in the world, within a matter of minutes based on long, sharp teeth. Hell, that same friend I've known since I was ten! My job as a dancing instructor came to an abrupt halt, leaving me unemployed, with no support from my parents because they disapproved of my dancing, and they now live in Australia. I have no other education because I focused on dance. I basically had no life, and I mean that literally, as I died soon after." Ivy pauses before sighing and looks at me. "It's truly a shame you witnessed wars and death in front of your eyes. I won't lie, glad it wasn't me to see those things happen. It's just you talk like you're the only one who has a grim outlook on life. Or angry at the way your life turned out. Everyone out there has a story. It's part of life. But we're here together, on a journey to see what happens when I meet the Vampire King. I could implement your ideas, make him see reason, and change paths for everyone. You have me as company, too!"

I open my mouth and close it, processing her

words. My hands grip the steering wheel again, all the tension returning. I expected her life to be easy, all rainbows and sunshine based on what I saw in her apartment, not what she's just explained. Then she spins it into trying to find something positive? I stopped seeing anything positive and better since my mother turned me away when I was trying to help her.

No, after I met Connor. Right, that's when I realized life is shit and I am living in hell on earth.

My quiet demeanor is enough for her to see my surprise. "Yeah, speechless, aren't you? I would be too." Ivy frowns and twirls her hair. "I bet you thought I had the sun shining from my ass and had everything handed to me on a silver platter. But unfortunately, I wasn't that lucky."

"I'm sorry... I admit, I misjudged you," I say slowly, putting on my best apologetic tone.

"Anyway, let's move on from this banter. It's just going to turn to be a 'who is more depressing' game." She pauses and sinks against the seat. "Actually, my mood for chatting has diminished." She then goes to grab her cell and curses as she shoves it back into her pocket. "Battery is low, so let's just sit and listen to the radio."

"Okay."

Reaching toward the dashboard, I switch on the radio, which blares out "Summer of 69" by Bryan Adams. Ivy just taps her foot to the music, and rather than it annoying me, I find my fingers tapping against the steering wheel in tune. Apart from that, the atmosphere in the car is suffocating, neither of us in a mood to talk. The cloud hanging above my head has now grown and sits above both of us.

But the green sign up ahead saying Laguna Beach makes me feel a little lighter, knowing we are close to the safe haven.

Chapter Fifteen

IVY

I swear, is it a guy thing or just a Zachary thing to ruin a pleasant moment? Getting to know each other is all I wanted to do after he made me mind-numbingly horny.

But no, let's get all grouchy and morbid. And then he has the audacity to assume I am a little princess that never had a depressing moment in her life. Argh!

Giving him a side glance, I notice his expression looks stoic. He's so closed off now. I want to know what he's thinking too, which annoys me, considering I'm the one that told him I'm not in the mood to talk.

Now, sitting beside him, I close my eyes and rehash the feeling of his body against mine. How his touch makes me feel wild and invigorated. The compulsion worked at the beginning, but as soon as his silky, delicious blood hit my tongue, I woke up from the daze. As much as I wanted to rip myself from him, I couldn't.

There was an intense connection as soon as my fangs sliced into his vein, and I felt glued to him. With each swallow of his blood, it spurred me on, making my mind obsessed with his taste. Although, I won't tell him this titbit of information. He will use it to his advantage by not compelling me anymore, and that's something I still prefer. It's just when in motion, it's hard to stop and I would rather enjoy that feeling than the beginning of piercing his skin. I had to pretend to stop—controlling myself as I submit to his command, though. Some part of me didn't want to listen and continue, but things were getting out of hand.

Fuck, it's all twisted. Why did Zachary have to be so attractive? So delicious to look at and tasty to drink.

I glance at him again, and I swear his eyes were on me too because he just as quickly returned his focus to the road.

Something is linking us together, and I know it's going to build stronger. Seldom does my gut steer me wrong. Regardless of my heightened senses, this is something personal. Something I know will happen regardless of how detached we try to be.

I purse my lips and shuffle back against the car seat. The only thing that's getting me through this awkward drive is the music.

Chapter Sixteen

ZACHARY

We finally arrived at Laguna Beach. I haven't been here before, but have heard that it's a coastal destination and worth seeing. Not that I would have ever come here before meeting Ivy. It's just an observation.

Overall, the drive wasn't as bad as I thought it would be. Luckily, during the trip, Ivy ended up forgetting the whole discussion when she heard a cheery pop song and got lost in it. It was a pleasant change to see her smile, as well as a bouncy attitude as she sang to the lyrics. I couldn't hide my grin, loving this new demeanor.

Once I find a spot in the private parking area, I switch off the car with the key card. As soon as it turns off, Ivy opens the door and practically leaps out of the car.

"Finally!" Ivy stands and stretches her arms, first lifting them above her head, which, fortunately for me, gives me an exquisite view of her cleavage. Then she bends down and touches her toes, flexing them one by one, and again, the two pillows are on display for me.

Dammit. She's a tease without even knowing it!

My cheeks puff as I exhale, failing at shrugging off the image of her body and the cheerfulness that clings to my brain. Maybe it likes it too much and wants to hold on to that pretty vision. "Hey, it wasn't that long of a drive. We're also lucky there aren't many people around, so that gives us privacy." I give a quick perusal of the empty area and point toward the apartments. "Stella owns a studio here, but it's part of another three units a developer designed after purchasing a knockdown house. From the looks of it, either the rest are vacant or the people who live here are at work."

"Stella sure seems invested in helping you," Ivy says, raising an eyebrow at me with a coy expression.

Ah yes, I know where her mind is going. And the answer is no.

I shake my head, then raise an eyebrow back at her. "Why would you care? Now *you* seem invested in my personal life." Ivy rolls her eyes, but I continue just to quench her curiosity, which is also entertaining. "Stella and I have been friends for almost a century and hadn't even crossed that friend zone. Not even a slip up. I have somewhat of a tie to her. I can sense her and...well, I never saw her anything more than the woman who saved me and continued to help me from that day." After finishing my explanation, I see a flash of emotion in her eyes. It isn't a happy one either. Jealousy, maybe? Regardless, this topic is irrelevant, and I don't want to go on about it. We need to dump our bags inside and start figuring out the fighting exercises I promised I'd teach. "Anyway, go grab your bag and follow me. The studio is the furthest one from this lot."

Ivy nods, and I sense her walking behind me. Her demeanor has now changed from the sarcasm and bouncy attitude she had only minutes ago.

Once we make our way to the studio apartment, we

pause at the door. It doesn't have a lock, but a code system. I haven't seen anything like it before as I press the digits Stella sent me. The door makes a click and I open it.

"Woah. I wasn't expecting such tech on a door," Ivy says. We're further surprised when we enter inside as the lights switch on automatically, offering us an amazing state-of-the-art lighting system.

"Stella sure loves her technology for an aged witch," I mumble, and Ivy nods in agreement.

The room looks pristine. I get the idea of a haven, but never understood why buy something extravagant like this studio and not live in it.

"Wow, this place looks stunning," Ivy exclaims as she walks past me to the middle of the room. She stands there, glancing around admiring the room, and I can understand her impressed look as it's quite a large room for a studio.

Stunning she says. If only I could tell her that it's not as stunning as you. But alas, this is something that's best not spoken as her knowing this may change her view toward me. I don't need attachments. Actually, we both don't need attachments.

Then suddenly, my appreciative thoughts are disrupted when I hear Ivy's surprise turn incredulous. "Hold on, there's no couch here?"

"Maybe Stella had this place in mind for more than sitting on the couch and reading a book," I quirk, raising my eyebrows up and down as I gesture toward the bed.

Ivy's jaw drops with a horrified expression. "Eww! Do you think the bed covers have even changed? No way am I sleeping on random bodily fluid."

"Relax, I was just kidding. This place looks unused, but if you're unconvinced, I'll be the gentleman to inspect it for you. Besides, I'm happy to sleep on the floor."

I hear her sigh and mumble something in response, which I quickly dismiss.

I lift the silky bedsheets, even the mattress, inspecting them as promised, knowing they were clean and untouched. "Nope, it's clean." I pick up the bag Ivy dropped onto the carpet when she pranced into the room, plonking it onto the bed, giving the mattress a light bounce.

"Thanks for that. But, uh, are you sure you want to sleep on the floor? I mean, the bed isn't a plank of wood." Ivy shrugs.

"Plank of wood?" I raise my eyebrow and give her a bemused grin.

Her eyes widen as she guffaws. "Come on, you know the scene? Titanic? Rose holds onto a plank of wood and rather than offering Jack to hold on beside her, he floats in the freezing water…"

I'm hearing her words, knowing exactly what she was talking about and at the same time, trying really hard not to laugh. Well, maybe not hard enough.

I shake my head and burst into laughter as I sit on the bed. "I have never met a vampire so invested in using a Hollywood film based on the *Titanic* as an analogy. The incredulous look on your face when you assumed I never watched the film… wish I took a photo."

Ivy narrows her eyes and pouts before she quips at me. "Well, you looked so dumbstruck, I assumed you didn't… ah, whatever." She gestures her hands in the air. "Moving on. Bed or floor?"

I stand, walk over to her, and rest my hand on her shoulder. "Look, the key priority is to get you fit enough to protect yourself. To decide where to sleep isn't an important issue." Whilst she doesn't show it, I feel her shudder the moment my hand touches her shoulder.

Hmm, interesting. She likes it.

Her reaction makes me want to test a theory to see if she is as taken by me as I am with her. Placing my other hand on her shoulder, she shudders again and admittingly, I enjoy the effect I have on her. It feels like a tug of war within me—wanting to be close to her but then pulling away because I know it's not meant to be. It sickens me and makes me envious at the same time. Twisted, I know, but fuck it, it's how I feel.

For decades, I've done my best to hold on to my humanity. Not that there haven't been downfalls in the past, though. Then again, surrendering to my lust is a downfall too, isn't it? Taking something that you know you'll never have a future with. To give false information or omitting the truth when you are going crazy with lust for someone. Developing, dare I say, feelings?

But fuck, she's so beautiful…

"You think I'm beautiful?" Ivy's voice sings out to me.

Shit! Did I just say that out loud?

Her surprise is visible even behind that gleeful smile. Even though I hadn't intended on admitting I found her beautiful, I can't help but answer her incredulous question. "What? You think you aren't? Come on, surely you look in the mirror, Ivy."

She exhales, then shrugs her shoulders. "Believe it or not, no one has ever said that to me. Only my parents called me beautiful, but that's coming from parents. Not the same thing when you hear it from someone else. Damien just called me terms of endearments, which was different."

Well, hell, I'm surprised at the confession. It's bewildering at how no one showered her with compliments and affection. I may not know her well, but I still see a sweet woman whose life has turned upside down. Whatever happens to Ivy, hopefully she holds on to her humanity.

I think about how to articulate the words and finally say, "Well, you are. And—"

"I can't believe it took me to die to hear those words." Ivy laughs before letting out a sigh. She places her hand on mine, blushing at the contact. "Thank you, Zachary. I may have pale skin, have aching gums that shoot out sharp fangs, but I'm still a human at heart and appreciate everything you have done for me. I'll try not to give you such a hard time, I promise!"

And then my cell phone rings.

The loud ringtone catches Ivy off guard, and she hastily removes her hand. Her sexy cheekbones are a painted pink tinge, bashful from my earlier comment, I presume. It's nice to know I can make her blush.

Hoping not to show my annoyance at the interruption, I casually pick up the cell and say, "Hi, Stell. Thanks for the studio. We are just settling in and then we'll head off to the beach when it gets dark outside. Luckily, our eyesight is phenomenal in the dark."

"Good. She needs to know what she will deal with.

On another note, a vision recently hit me. Not the best timing. It happened during a reading I was doing for a customer." I clearly heard the gruffiness in his tone. "The Gray Clan are figuring out how to approach this situation you and Ivy are in. If you had longer, I'd suggest showing her how to use guns, but that doesn't seem likely. Just make sure she can understand and deal with her new abilities. Yes, it sounds pushy and repetitive, but in all seriousness, she needs to be prepared for Connor. Her beauty aside, he will also be pleased with a tough and strong Queen." There is a pause though, despite sounding like the spiel was finished.

What else does she know?

"Is there more you'd like to add, Stell? I sense it."

Stella sighs. "Damn, I keep forgetting that. Look, I didn't really want to dwell on it, but I have a gut feeling that all these visions are part of a grand gesture that will happen soon. There is a saying within the witch's coven, which I am part of being a seer, is that when we get multiple visions of the same thing or situation, it can be a sign that we need to prepare. That whatever it is we're seeing, will haunt us until it's finished. Which is why I am pushing for you to make sure you're ready for a fight."

"I'm still confused why you can't see exactly what will happen. Or at least find out more about the Prophecy."

Stella breathes out a sigh. "I tried, I did some readings, trying to figure out what the future holds and by that, I mean, a full vision. No snippets here and there, like I am having now. It's bizarre... and come to think of it, they began when I first met you. Remember when I said I had a vision, but you dismissed me, so I never told you?"

I scoff at her question, a little too arrogantly, but it's not every day when someone questions an immortal's memory. A vampire has the capacity for an amazing memory. "Yes, I remember. I was too preoccupied with…" I don't say exactly what I want to because Ivy is in the room. "Doesn't matter, what's the point? Are you saying that you saw visions all those years ago?"

"Well, I tried to tell you, but you refused to hear it, so I dropped it. Anyway, that was the second time my third eye called. Ever since then, whenever I want a vision, or even don't want one, it comes in flashes but never the whole story," Stella says with a hint of confusion in her voice. It almost makes me feel bad, to have a strong Seer doubt her own magical ability. "It doesn't matter though, because I believe you need to take this seriously."

I let out a curse, annoyed with the escalation. This situation is growing more serious than anticipated. "Fuck, okay. This is becoming a vampire saga. I wish you would have told me this earlier, though. There aren't many secrets between us, and this is something that you should have divulged. Anyway, I'll stay here with Ivy for two days and help her out, and then we'll drive up to see Co—the Vampire King straight away." Lowering my voice, I add, "So far, he hasn't contacted me, so that's a good thing. Hopefully, the quicker we get to Santa Monica, the better so we can outrun these wolves. The mutts want Ivy, and I'm going to make sure they don't get close." I pause for a moment, realizing that a hint of protectiveness appeared in my tone. It wasn't protective for the sake of getting her to Connor. I have a feeling that it's my emotions toward her that are making me defensive.

I sense some movement behind me, and turn to see Ivy standing there, with her mesmerizing amber eyes watching me, full of curiosity. For someone who has fangs and bit into me ferociously only hours ago, her eyes boast innocence and the facial expression matching.

I snap back to the conversation with Stella. "Anyway, thanks for everything. Sorry if I sounded gruff, but there's a lot happening. Don't know what I'd be doing without your help. Keep me in the loop. I'll chat with you later."

Ending the call, I shove my cell back into my pocket.

"I assume that was Stella, your witch friend? What did she see?" Ivy asks as she steps closer to me.

"Yes, that was her."

I explain what Stella foresaw and how I assume it's going to be an attack on us. I skip the discussion about Stella's third eye though, but give enough facts for her to understand why Stella called and urges us to move.

Ivy's eyes furrow and her disposition turns quiet, surprising me when she nods and says, "Okay, then we better get this training started. I'll do whatever you want me to do." She moves a little closer to me, surprising me by placing her hand gently on my arm. "I also want to thank you for what you said to Stella...about not letting the wolves get to me. I haven't had someone feel protective of me for a while. The one person I wanted that from is the leader of the pack who wants me dead." She stays in place, not moving away to give distance as I would have expected her to. But rather than look me in the eye, she lowers her head. And then it hits me. She's thinking about Damien. Likely to be remembering their time together. A part of me is jealous, but knowing what Damien did to her, or rather did not do, I know she wouldn't forgive him.

Despite the envy about her thoughts of Damien, my mouth forms a smile and words that haven't been uttered to someone since my parents passed away fly out unhindered. "No matter what, I'll protect you, Ivy."

I don't know why I said that, or if I should have said it at all, but it was the truth. With my brain getting foggy by her touch, I finally regain my focus. *Training, that's where I need to direct my energy toward.*

I softly pat her hand, still resting on my arm. "Anyway, let's head out to the beach and see what you can do with your body." In perfect timing, unison you could say, we both freeze in realization about how provocative it sounded.

Ivy raises her eyebrows and gives me a playful smile. "What's that supposed to mean?"

I swear, my skin probably turned several shades paler. The words flew out of my mouth, making a fool of myself. Then again, her eyes speak of something else other than surprise at the comment. The twinkle in her eyes swirls with curiosity and intrigue. *Maybe she likes the sound of that just as much as I do?*

"Sorry, I didn't mean it that way. What I meant was that I want to see how you can use your body to defend yourself."

Ivy giggles and waves her hand in a 'don't worry about it' gesture. "I know what you meant. It's fine. Besides, I've been dancing for many years and feel confident that I'm fit enough to learn the moves to defend myself. I promise to be your best pupil," she says, batting her eyelashes.

I grin and gesture her toward the door. "Well, I'll believe it when I see it."

Her reaction is quick as she strides out the door and says, "Challenge accepted."

Chapter Seventeen

ZACHARY

Our feet sink into the soft sand as we walk around, finding a spot to mark as ours. The moonlight makes her skin stand out, and fuck, she is stunning. My cock twitches. It has a mind of its own when it's attracted to a body that makes your head fog up with indecent thoughts.

How many times can my dick say 'well, hello there!' when I look at her? Even now, she stands in front of me, hands on her waist, waiting to be told what to do. And I can't help to muster back a grin, loving her expression. Those orbs holding mine, ready for whatever I throw her way.

"So, what now?"

The fog that had my brain drowning in thoughts of Ivy's attraction disappears.

Walking toward her, I meet her inches away when she stills, not expecting me to get that close. She takes a deep breath and waits for my answer.

Instead, I lean in, a whisper away from her ear and say, "Run."

Her eyes widen, no doubt in surprise. "What? I don—" But she doesn't finish the sentence as she cries in horror.

My face now contorts in what a true vision of a

vampire is, especially one who is ready to pounce. Ivy hasn't seen it before, but I know what we look like. It's the same for all vampires—thick black veins flowing from the sides of the eyes. They change into a deep red, just like I described to her earlier. My fangs are out, sharp, and look just as angry as my face does. I want to terrify her. Even if she is a vampire herself, they can also live in fear, not knowing about other vampires who can be ten times scarier and ruthless predators. I was one of them under Connor's control at one point, but after a decade of being the true monster, gave in to the voice in my head telling me this was wrong.

I keep reminding myself that it was a long time ago, and as the years turned into decades, research improved and so did ways of being a vampire in the modern world. I chose blood bags.

In no time, Ivy was already speeding away from me, and I can sense her shock, but what surprises me is that I also sense a hint of excitement. Her endorphins rising indicate this is going to be an interesting session. I spring after her, even though her speed is fast for a vampire, I'm still faster. She screeches to a halt, slamming into my chest as I appear in front of her, holding both her shoulders to help keep her balance.

"Good, at least we know you can run fast, but you'll need to practice and learn to be faster. And next time, if I say run, please listen and disappear. No questions asked. You are a predator. You chase your prey. It's now in your nature and keep in mind, it's *when*, not *if*, others will come to attack you."

She narrows her eyes and shrugs my hands off, stepping back. "Hey! You blindsided me. I was in shock! And your face... hell, is that what I look like too?" Ivy covers her eyes and for a few seconds, I fear she will burst into tears. But surprisingly, she just shakes her head and places her hands on her hips. "Hey, why did you begin with running, not throwing a punch or kick? You could have pummelled me or punched me in the throat," she asks, her fingers touching her neck. But rather than fear of the brute move, instead, I see intrigue settling over her facial expression.

I give her a grin, proud that she noticed that detail. "Glad you pointed that out. I started with that for a couple of reasons. First, I wanted to see how fast you can run, to gauge your abilities you now have. Second, being that running will be the best way to get out of a position if you don't need to physically fight off an enemy. If you're worried about the situation or see that disappearing would be the ideal way to avoid them, running is the best choice. Perhaps a pussy way out of the situation, but for now, with you being so newly transformed, it's the easy choice."

Ivy stands there with her mouth open and closing, reminding me of a fish. I can barely contain a chuckle, clearly leaving her speechless with my reasoning.

Even though she wants a heads-up on what I plan on doing, I don't like that method. When you're in a fight, no one is going to help. They are there to either weaken their opponent, or kill them.

"Okay, that's fair enough. Good thinking!"

A chuckle vibrates out of my chest. "Thanks. It's good to know you agree with my decisions. You'll get quicker and swifter as you grow stronger. It's all about balancing that you're now super-fast added by new strength and endurance."

"That won't take too long for me. I don't mean to

be tooting my own horn, but my body is used to enduring physical activity with all the dancing and training I did. I think that might be an extra benefit if I need to fight."

I'm not sure if Ivy is waiting for me to say something, but I can't form words because my naughty brain is still grasping onto the 'enduring physical activity' part.

"Ah, Zachary?" Ivy says with a perfectly plucked, raised eyebrow.

I jerk back, realizing I was standing here drooling over her words.

Shit, I really need to get my head out of the gutter.

"How about you throw a punch at me?"

Her eyebrows bunch, and then she glances at her hands, forming them into a fist. "But I haven't punched anyone before. I don't know what I'll be doing."

"Are you going to comment on everything I ask you to do? Seriously, just punch me. You won't hurt me because I'll duck way before you think you might hit me," I say with a smirk, liking the way she gives me a challenging glare. Maybe I need to push her buttons in order to shut her up and get her to show me moves.

"Fine, but don't be pissed off if I do end up hitting you," she sputters and throws her fist toward my chest. It doesn't touch my skin though, as predicted. I move out of the way the moment her hand moves toward me. I do sense the force in the punch, though. If it did ever hit someone, it would knock them back a little, depending on their strength, of course. I expect her to stop, but the woman who uses film analogies actually catches me by surprise. I feel a whack in my chest, the punch vibrating through my ribs. It doesn't stop after that one hit either. Like a robot, she continues throwing punch after punch, and I finally duck the last few. The nonstop punching and smug grin on her face begins to frustrate me, so I give her a maneuver she won't expect. Ducking her next punch, I get low to the ground and sweep my foot out, knocking her ankle with a force that makes her wobble and fall back. Not very gracefully, either.

"Ouch," Ivy grumbles as she sits on her cute ass, her amber eyes throwing daggers at me.

I offer my hand, feeling bad that I hurt her, but realize it's not the best idea because I need to make her angry enough to follow my instructions. Pushing her buttons is what needs to be done to get attention. I lower my hand and shove it in my pocket. "Your punches were great—strong with lots of force. The more you did, the swifter they became, so I'm happy with that. It'll come in handy when you need to hit an opponent, even just to knock them back. At first, Supernatural creatures won't be affected too much by your punches like humans would be, but it's something that can surprise them. Being sated also helps immensely when fighting."

Ivy nods and gets up from the sand where she landed from my kick. Patting away the sand from her clothes, she says, "I sensed that you hesitated for a second after the first punch. That's why I kept punching until I hit you. I now understand the 'heightened senses' part."

I grin, happy that she grasps the concept of heightened senses and used that at an opportune moment. "Good. Next up, can you tell me how high you can lift your leg?"

She bursts out in a chuckle, meeting my own as I realize my question sounds odd and unexpected. It also intrigues me, curious how flexible she can be.

"Why do you need me to demonstrate how high I can lift my leg, Zachary?"

"Show me, Ivy. It's got to do with a high kick. Happy?"

"Oh, okay." With a quick nod, she lifts her right leg in the air, her left foot balancing perfectly on the sand. Suddenly, I have an image of her as a ballerina, delicate but with a mind full of dedication. Beautiful, and ready for flight. "Is this alright? I can go higher but I don't think that's going to help my cause."

I swallow, my Adam's apple bopping up and down as I watch her lift her leg up in the air. "Yeah, that's fine. You can put your leg back down." I pause and clear my throat before continuing. "Now, I want to see you kick. Similar to how you threw punches, do a free-standing kick. Improvise, it doesn't matter. But when you do, use force and kick upward. The aim, at least from my experience, is to kick them high in the air. Make them fly away from you rather than come at you. Get the gist?"

"Okay." She straightens her shoulders and stretches her toes while adjusting her stance.

"One, two, three!" I count loudly.

At three, I watch her run toward me and momentarily stop and kick her leg up high, missing me by inches. I move out of the way the moment she stops, which is a move that I consider a waste of time. Even a mistake in my opinion. Another vampire would have done the same, so that won't work.

"Crap," Ivy grumbles, losing balance as she

realizes she didn't hit me.

"Don't stop, or even hesitate. When you run toward them, the aim is to surprise." I speed up to her and by the time she can take a deep breath, my boot is already positioned against her neck. The move isn't to scare her, but rather to make her understand she needs to surprise or shock her opponent. I put my leg back down and take a step away from Ivy, who is rubbing her neck as if I had hit her there.

"Again," she announces, regaining her concentration, still eager to get the kick right. Most importantly, I notice the black veins creep from the side of her eyes, like thick crow's feet, and the glint of sharp fangs. Good, she's angry. She needs to be in the right mindset to fight, not cheeky banter.

I move back, giving enough distance for her to run and aim a kick at me. Before I can say one, she is practically in front of me. Her foot connects with my chest and I'm flying in the air. It wasn't that far, but forceful enough to have me land on the sand a couple of meters away. Still, very impressive.

"Yes!" Ivy throws some air punches and does what humans call a 'happy dance'. The impact of her kick has me land on my ass, but I stop myself from getting up. Instead, I watch her face grow back to normal, her hips shimmying from side to side as she does a Rocky Balboa fist pump in the air. In a happy moment, Ivy looks gorgeous and I'm glad that I get the chance to see her like this. From the get-go, it's all been morbid, about blood, being a 'monster', death, and fighting. Even in the car when we could have had a pleasant conversation, it grew depressing and led to a tense situation. Right now, I see her in a different light, and pleased it's because of me.

Snapping out of my stupor, I get up and brush the sand off my jeans. "You did well, Ivy. Even though you negated all my instructions, you really picked up and showed you are adapting to the abilities." Walking over to her, she suddenly stills, looking a little startled. I inwardly chuckle at her expression. Obviously, she wasn't expecting me to watch her happy dance.

She laughs nervously. "You saw that, didn't you?"

I grin. As a vampire, everyone probably doubts we can be happy, but I can't stop grinning when I'm around Ivy. It's almost cringe-worthy.

"Crap, how embarrassing," she mumbles, even though I heard it clearly.

"Hearing. That's another thing I need to mention." I point to my ear and say, "We can hear very well. You might as well say things loud and clear because there is no point in trying to hide your words. You have nothing to be embarrassed about. It was very cute."

Ivy laughs, and then adds, "Plus, I was totally badass and actually threw you off guard." Lifting her fingers toward her mouth, she pretends to blow smoke.

I roll my eyes at her teasing, and then suddenly an idea pops into my mind. One that I know will throw her off guard. It may seem immature, but I like to think of it as part of her training.

"So, how are you adapting to the eyesight in the dark?"

"It's all right. The sensation is a bit odd, but I'm getting used to it. It's been unusual since I first transformed, even back at the apartment." Ivy shrugs.

"That's good, and I assume the heightened state of sensing things around you is fine too?"

"Yeah, guess so…" She trails off. "Hey, do you think I can go check out the water before we head back to the apartment? The workout was enough for today. I didn't stretch for a while and my body is still in pain. I want to take care of it, not push it to exertion." Ivy then pauses and furrows her brow. "I just realized how human that sounds. It's what I would say when I was dancing. Guess I don't need to stretch or worry about my body anymore…" Ivy glances up at me with an expression I don't know how to respond to.

Is she waiting for me to confirm?

I shrug because I don't know what to say.

Ivy rolls her eyes at my unhelpful gesture and nods toward the water.

"I'm going to go and relax for a few minutes."

"Sure, I'll just wait around for you."

Ivy gives me a half smile. "What, you scared someone is going to attack me? I can protect myself. Vampire or not, I'll be fine." She strolls away, heading toward the water. The reflection of the moon is catching as she stands, feet sinking into the sand. I don't see her walking toward the water any further though, just shuffling in the same spot, momentarily staring at her feet, wiggling her toes. As beautiful as the water shimmering in the moonlight is, it's nothing compared to how beautiful Ivy is.

Hell. How can fate make someone so innocent and beautiful turn into an evil creature?

But my stupor snaps off as the devil on my shoulder reminds me of my fun idea. In a blur, I appear behind her back and whisper, "Boo!"

As expected, Ivy screams in shock, caught off balance and falls into the water with a loud splash.

Now, she probably thinks I'm a douche, but I honestly have a good reason behind this, as well as wanting to demonstrate she can be caught off guard at any time. Call it pride, call it showing off, whatever, but within minutes, she just failed at using the ability to sense me behind her, or at least move out of the way. Ivy didn't even turn around, just stood there in her own world when in a matter of seconds, a powerful vampire, or any fast creature, could have snapped her neck.

Unfortunately, I did not predict a wave to approach her and, with the sudden impact, Ivy is pulled further away from the shallow spot she was in. Not sure where the waves came from, especially as it was peaceful before, but I can hear her squeal again. It's meant to be quiet and the water still, but the cruelty of the water swallowing her catches me off guard. Again.

"I can't swim! I'm terrified of drow—" Ivy squeals.

Fuck, she can't swim!?

I rush into the water, catching up to her. My feet sink in as an anchor and grab hold of Ivy, who is now drenched. With my arms wrapped around her waist, I yank her out, and in only a matter of a few long strides, we are back on the sand with her practically clinging to me like a koala.

I place her on the sand, pissed off at how my plan backfired.

"What the hell were you thinking of standing in the water if you can't swim?"

"W-what the hell were y-you thinking of by scaring me? I just wanted to dip my toes into the water, not g-go swimming. Are your bolts getting loose in your head?" Ivy says through chattering teeth as she stands there trembling.

My hands have a mind of their own as I rub her arms up and down, trying to calm her down. "I'm sorry. It was my fault. I just wanted to test you…if someone were to pounce, you would have been killed by now. You didn't turn or run…nothing. It was a human reaction to not retaliate or notice what's behind you before it's too late. I wanted to catch you off guard." I continue rubbing her and then her back, shoulders, and then I find my hands on her waist. And they stay there, even though I should remove them.

Fuck, what the hell am I doing?

Chapter Eighteen

IVY

I want to kill him for his dumbass prank. Although, the feel of his heated touch caressing my body feels amazing. Goose pimples appear right at his touch. There is no denying I'm attracted to him.

My eyes close as I give in to Zachary, affectionally attempting to warm me. I don't even know if that's possible, feeling all sorts of temperatures, but hell, it's driving me crazy. It's driving my nether regions mad with desire.

Doing all this training seems pointless to me, considering I won't be on a battlefield. Technically, I have no idea what's coming my way, but I doubt I require all this exercise. However, if Zachary thinks it's a good idea to have some knowledge of how to defend myself and use my new abilities, I might as well. If I must admit it, I want to be here with him. Being separated from him unnerves me. My body shudders at the thought.

Whilst I enjoy knowing I can do a few moves that aren't related to dancing, it still seems futile. I must admit, the satisfying feeling after getting a few punches at Zachary was a high point. Everything seems faster and swifter. Even my sight is edgier and fiercer, especially in the dark. It's bizarre.

Throughout everything, Zachary was like a hot teacher, eyes dark, serious, and dreamy. Determined to make me want to succeed. It was even cute how he held back on me, even though we both know that if anyone ever attacked me, they wouldn't hold back and cut me some slack.

Even after that silly stunt, I wrap myself in his magical scent. His touch is making everything fade away. My body is now warm, and I'm stifling moans from his wandering hands, even if all they are touching are my arms and shoulders.

I want them to move down further. I want more.

Woah, where did that thought come from? Ah crap, not again. I'm surrendering to him—his amazing emerald eyes, that perfect mouth, and hard body and...argh! Now I'm craving him.

The temptation makes me want to hammer down the barrier he puts up between us. I want to kick away the rubble and launch at him like a frickin' missile. But now I also wonder if the temptation is because I consumed his blood.

Chapter Nineteen

ZACHARY

Ivy seems to have settled down, shivering less than before, and I already notice her arms are drier. I'm just about to drop my hands from their sudden exploration when I look at her and find myself drowning in her expression. As she slowly glances down at my hands still placed on her waist, I feel her tremble. My traitorous fingers lightly caress her soft skin, feeling the smoothness as my thumbs move in gentle circles.

Her eyes are pools of heat and suddenly, two soft hands rest on my shoulders. We are close enough that I feel the shivering cease and now shuddering at my touch, clearly affected by the closeness of our bodies. My knees jerk at the thought that she didn't move away from me and instead reciprocated touching me.

I want to fight this lust. It's messing with my head, but I fail at composing myself because my lips curve into a smile. It won't hurt to revel in some of this chemistry we have. Ivy watches my reaction and rewards me with one of hers, lifting those pouty lips. The gesture surprises me, not at the top of the list of things I would expect her to do. After all the arguing, sarcastic banter, and yes, moments of bliss during feeds, she has never really hinted at her feelings.

Her sweet smile reminds me of a cherub, and I feel

like the arrow has certainly hit me. But along with that smile, there's a twinkle of affection in her eyes, which makes my cock say 'hello' again. This time, our bodies are close enough that she can feel it. It's embarrassing, but at the same time, I really don't want to think about that. I'm losing this emotional war between getting Ivy to Connor, using her as bait in my plan to erase Connor from my life versus taking her and keeping Ivy all to myself.

Her lusty eyes slowly roam my face and land on my lips. I can't help but gaze at her slim neck, finding that spot I pierced with my fangs. My eyes roam further, and I bite my lip as it lands on her soaking wet tank top, her two pert nipples that stand up in greeting.

Dick, meet nipples. You both seem to like to say hello.

Noticing where my eyes have landed, she drops her hands from my shoulder and straightens her back, giving a sliver of distance between us, as if she didn't want to move away. Ivy sighs, and I know from the look on her pinched expression, she wants to talk.

Great, not my strongest suit.

"Zachary, I don't know you very well," she whispers, "but the truth is that I crave you sometimes, and…well, I'm wondering if that's because I drank from you?"

Well, I never expected that question, and I also never thought about it from that angle.

"And what if it wasn't?" I ask because now I'm curious to know if she would find me attractive without the vampire factor.

Ivy bites down on her lower lip. "I guess I'm left in a predicament."

"What predicament would that be?" My tone is wary, yet I'm filled with intrigue.

The slight pause in her response shows her hesitance.

"Well, it means that I'm caught between craving you, with this crazy pull you hold over me. Or putting my attraction toward you as ridiculous. That the concept of me unraveling you is silly. Denying how I find it hard to keep thinking straight when you're always around. That I should focus on anything else, so you can do your job and bring me to the Vampire King."

And just like that, my mind becomes a whirlwind of chaos, knowing I have the identical dilemma. Whilst I'm trying to process and form words, I see the longing in her eyes. Waiting for my reaction, filled with lust and need. Moments like these are when I want someone else to decide things for me. I want her and I am attracted to her, but know this is going to be a dead end. Ironic, right?

Suddenly, her lips crash against mine, catching me off guard. When I realize she took the first step whilst I'm standing here, lost in my thoughts, my male prowess reappears from its hiatus, and I kiss her back.

My fingers lightly grasp her head, holding her still so I could properly taste her mouth, her tantalizing tongue, and even a gentle lick of the now lengthening fangs. Her fragrant scent surrounds me as I indulge in this moment.

Her long nails dig into my shoulders, holding on like she's drowning. It feels amazing. Not just kissing her, but to have her holding on to me so tightly proves how much she wants this. Whatever is happening between us, it's definitely not one-sided, and that pleases me.

Her lips are smooth, and then a drop of blood drips down from where I nip. Tastes like liquid lust. It's as if her blood expresses its feelings of arousal and yearning.

As I lick the decadent drop, I feel her mouth move into a smile. Ivy puts her hands in my hair and tugs me close. The intimacy between us is so strong. It's like a constant pull we have to each other. I don't know what it is, but it's confusing and threatening its false hope for both of us.

Ivy makes a loud sigh, sweet and sexy, but it was dramatic enough to make me pause the momentum of our kisses.

Slowly, I pull back, ending this delicious kiss, and try to get a grip before my actions go further. The surprise in her eyes makes me feel terrible because I know that I'm blindsiding her and she is like an innocent doe.

Chapter Twenty

ZACHARY

The wind kicks up, getting colder as the evening turns to midnight. I rub the back of my neck and notice Ivy's perfectly shaped eyebrows bunched in confusion.

"Did I do something wrong?" she asks quietly, self-consciousness in her tone.

Shit, I don't want her to think she did something wrong.

"No, no. Not at all." I put the loose strand of hair behind her ear and leave my hand there longer than needed. "It's just, well, it's been a long day. Let's call it a night, unless you'd rather practice a little?"

Technically, she doesn't really need to practice as she already picked up enough from earlier. I just need to divert her from me. One of us needs to be out of the equation to keep a cool mind.

"You're right. I think I'll do some practice whilst I can. We became side-tracked, and that's not what either of us needs. I'll see you soon." The smile falters, and she turns around swiftly. She speeds off into the darkness, leaving me standing alone on the sand.

Clearly, she's become accustomed to the rapid pace and eyesight that comes with the vampire package.

My boots sink into the soft sand as I look over at the horizon. My gaze travels aimlessly across the water, soaking in the fresh salty air. The scent of the ocean always fascinated me. Still, I'm here to watch over Ivy and despite enjoying the fresh air and peace, I glance around the beach innocuously, so she doesn't know I'm watching. Especially considering I stopped whatever was happening between us.

Oddly enough, I find her kicking a tree trunk.

What the hell is she doing?

It seems like Ivy's using it as a kicking bag, hitting the same spot again and again. She's focused and fierce, very sexy to watch. I notice the tree trunk literally move. Though the agility I've mastered over the decades has me over beside the trunk in less than a second.

"Any harder and it will split. Now, wouldn't that be an odd sight for humans to see?" I muse, leaning against the trunk, hoping she would stop and move on.

"Okay, I'll give it a break with the kicking. Now I can move on to the punches," she says determinately and does a few jabs and crosses, changing up the technique—which I didn't even show her. And then, what do you know? I hear a fucking crack.

Shit, she must be very strong. Stronger than I expected.

"Crap!" Ivy squeals and immediately stops. Her shriek is cute, so very opposite of the tough exterior she is putting on.

"Great, that's exactly what we need…" I mutter.

I take a quick look at Ivy to see her reaction. She's frozen, standing with her hands covering her face. Ivy finally shakes her head and lowers her hands, letting me see the unease and mortification in her expression.

"Let's just call it a night," she suggests, and starts

Tania Gold

walking toward the direction of the studio, but stops and does a three-hundred-sixty-degree turn.

Ivy steps closer to the tree trunk and whispers sorry as she gives it a light pat. She turns to me and gives me an apologetic smile before disappearing toward the studio.

She doesn't see it but as she disappears, a chuckle breaks out of me. Ivy reminds me of a kitten—cute and adorable but with claws sharp enough to slice you. Can be great to snuggle with but can leave you with bleeding cuts if angered.

And of course, I'm a cat person.

The lights are on by the time I arrive back at the studio. Pride surges through my chest as I recall the past hour. Looks like I underestimated her—not only is she sharp and strong, she also has mastered her ability to use speed to escape prey. A disappearing act in the blink of an eye added to it swift punches that come out of nowhere. A dangerous combination to have and she'll only get faster, stronger, and fiercer as time goes by.

Chapter Twenty-One

ZACHARY

Once inside the spacious studio, I see her laying on the bed, head plopped on the pillow as she stares at the ceiling.

I lean against the blinding white wall, cross my arms, admiring her. But not for long, as her voice shatters the silence.

"Staring at someone is considered rude, you know?" Ivy exclaims, with a hint of amusement in her tone.

A chuckle vibrates through my chest, loving the sarcasm.

"Knowing someone is in the room and blatantly ignoring them is also considered rude, *you know*," I quip, playful humor in my tone.

I sliver of a smile appears. "*Touché.*"

Ivy sighs and rolls to her side, elbow on the mattress, and chin cupped in her palm. "Sleep in the bed, it's fine. Besides, we already kissed and...well, I also have a feeling you're trying to avoid doing anything further with me. Anyway, make yourself comfortable. I won't bite." She then rolls onto her back and chuckles at her own words. "Ah, the irony."

Nodding, I walk over, sit, and take off my leather boots then jacket. If I knew what I was getting myself into, I would have packed extra items. Probably a tad more colorful casual clothing rather than looking like the grim reaper.

I still have some soul left in me. There surely is some light inside... isn't there?

I shake off the depressing thought and remove my shirt, but stop there. I'm used to sleeping in my boxers, but tonight I think keeping on some clothes is the best choice. Even if I can see her trying hard not to stare at my bare chest.

Is she actually eye fucking me?

"You like what you see?" The words fly out without the intention of sounding cocky. But now they're out there, I'm intrigued to hear her response. If she asked me that same question, the answer would straight up be, "Yes."

Ivy clears her throat and shrugs, despite her pink cheeks. She sits up, leans over the night dresser, and switches off the lamp. The darkness envelopes us, but my eyesight is still as healthy as it is during the day. I watch her lie back down and stretch out her body, trying to find a comfortable position. It reminds me of a cat, taking its time until it finds a position to curl up into.

"Hey, Zachary...can I ask you something?" she asks, startling me out of my gaze.

"Sure," I respond, curiosity enticing me.

"What's your story?"

"What do you mean by that?"

"Like, before you turned into a vampire. Tell me about Zachary."

My history isn't my favorite topic, but with all the half-truths and omissions, she deserves to at least know something about me.

"Well, I was born into a middle-class family in Los Angeles. My parents were humble people, yet I guess we still enjoyed the decadent things in life when we were able to." I smile, remembering the times when Father returned from trips with silk dresses for Mother, or the time when he bought me my pocket watch. It was all the rage at the time and only the wealthy had them. "To be honest, all I cared about was to have a family that was happy and healthy. I know it doesn't sound like something I would say, but that's what I was like. Hard to believe it's almost one hundred years ago now."

"That's very sweet of you to want to have that, though. At least that's my opinion. Did you have any siblings?"

Crap. Just as I was getting to the concept of being honest with her, she asks me this question. I purse my lips, stuck at the response I should give. *Do I twist the truth again?*

I clear my throat. "Ah, not that I know of. I grew up being an only child, only me around, which I can admit was lonely at times."

Ivy lets out a deep sigh. "Yeah, me too. I always wanted to have another person in my family I could confide in. Like a best friend who shared blood and a tight friendship. I don't think my mother could conceive easily, making me the miracle child. Only, she never spoke about it. It's just something I grew up thinking."

"Mmm." I focus on a spot on the ceiling, thinking how shocked I was to find out I had a twin brother. He broke my heart just like Mother did. Maybe it would have been better to have never met him. My life would be so different.

I feel a shift on the bed and return from my reverie. "Just because a family has the same blood running in their DNA, it doesn't necessarily mean it runs thicker than water. The saying is a bunch of lies, in my opinion. My mother turned me away and didn't want to have anything to do with me. This...monster." I pause at the image of Mother slaying me with hurtful words. "That's what she called me when all I wanted to do was to help heal her. It was only then I found out about the monster I was going to become. At least she warned me about the pain," I finish with a mutter.

"I know pity is the last thing you want to hear, and I don't pity you, but I am sorry that you had to go through that. Seeing them die and being helpless... I hate hearing that you had such a good heart and now..." Ivy doesn't finish, leaving the rest of the sentence hanging in the air. The tone of her voice hitches as I know there is something behind her words, but I won't push to know more.

Instead of trying to decipher what she wanted to say, I move on and settle with honesty.

"I wouldn't wish it upon anyone."

I thought silence would come next, but I could sense Ivy wide awake and knew there was going to be more.

"Ivy, I can sense you thinking," I say with a lopsided grin.

"Ahh. Yes, I forgot you can anticipate how I feel," she says with a giggle.

Giving her a verbal nudge, I say, "What else is on your mind?"

"You never asked about my background. My story," she answers in a hushed tone.

"You mean, pre-life-sucks-and-I'm-a-vampire-now?"

Ivy bursts out in laughter. "Yeah, all that." She finishes with a badly restrained giggle.

"So, what's the story pre-transition?"

She shuffles, making the mattress move until she finds a comfortable position and then makes a deep sigh.

"My parents are very unconventional people. I wouldn't say hippies like in the 70s, but free enough to make other people notice. I was teased by their behavior and tried to not let them put their values onto mine. Great people, and very loving toward me. There were times where I thought it was mainly because I was the only child. I mean, every child has their insecurities."

"Well, it's good to know that you had a loving family. Not everyone gets a close unit when it comes to families and having a sibling doesn't always bring on… good relationships with them. Sometimes all anyone needs is a good friend to rely on. Stella is like the only family I have in some way. Not technically a sibling but, has been a part of my life since the time I transitioned. Anyway, like I said, you don't need a blood relative to be the most reliable person in your life."

The mattress moves again. This time she sits up and looks at me.

"Damien was my closest friend. I loved him, at first like a brother, but there were times as we reached twenty where it felt like…more, I guess. We were through a lot over the years. We actually met when we were ten. Both newbies at, okay please don't laugh... band camp."

I laugh. Sorry, but that's a funny thing to envision, sexy vampire Ivy at band camp. The mattress shakes due to my larger frame, and then I receive a light shove on the shoulder.

"I told you not to laugh!" she exasperates.

"Sorry, sorry. Okay, continue." I suppress a chuckle and gesture with my hands to continue.

"Anyway, that's where we first met and over the years, we learned how to play instruments, and then soon afterward I decided to do dancing instead. Poor guy wasn't happy to be left behind with all the other band nerds." Ivy laughs to herself, clearly thinking of the good times. Though her mood shifts and I sense a sadness within her, she lets out a deep sigh and says, "Actually, sorry, I don't want to talk about this part. It just hurts thinking about it. Being friends with someone for over a decade is a long time to just be frickin' turned away from. Shit, Zachary, I'm so pissed off at him!" Ivy snaps and punches the mattress in frustration, which I guess is better than a tree.

I don't want to see her upset so I try to divert the topic and gently grab her hand to stop its aggressiveness.

"What made you like dancing so much? I've never been able to dance." Her hand stills beneath mine and I let it go, but she doesn't notice as she laughs, the charming sound echoing throughout the room.

"I'd love to see you try! Now I understand why you laughed at me when I mentioned band camp. The image of us doing something so out of our present character is sort of amusing. And to answer your question, I always loved to dance. The concept that music can make a body do so many various movements intrigued me. Plus, as an added bonus, I was flexible and just loved moving to music. Apparently, when I was a toddler, I used to stand in front of buskers and was one of those kids that swayed to the music, clapping along to the tune. As the years went on, swaying turned to performing some steps and well, then Mom decided to enroll me in a dancing school," Ivy says nonchalantly.

"Guess you're lucky she did that. It seems like it was a good decision."

"Yeah, but I think she saw it as a hobby, not really as a future. Everything was fine up until I was eighteen and finished senior year. Then it was like dancing was a no-no." I hear the annoyance in Ivy's tone.

"Well, on the bright side, it gave you an opportunity to teach dancing."

Ivy opens her mouth to say something but stills as my phone vibrates.

"Stella," we say in unison, although mine is confirming and Ivy's more of a question.

Hi Zach, I forgot to mention that there are some blood bags in the mini fridge. They're not fresh, so don't get too excited. I had a friend store them for you once I found out that you would head over there. Try not to chug them down too quickly! Stell.

My lips quirk, missing her sarcasm, or how she admonishes me when I do the wrong things. Then again, as my gaze goes back to Ivy, I realize she does exactly the same thing. The difference is that I find it deliciously attractive when it comes from her.

"What did she say?" Ivy asks with a hint of urgency.

Putting the phone on silent, I chuck it on the nightstand and say, "Blood bags are in the fridge. Not fresh, but better than nothing, so let's check it out before we get hungry again. This time, I have nothing else to change into if it gets dirty." I chuckle and give a pointed look toward her. "And this time it's best you don't drink from me. Not sure if too much of my blood will get you sort of addicted, but you are already becoming a fiend." I chuckle and then add, "It's very...hot."

Instead of hearing something sarcastic from Ivy, I hear silence. The elephant in the room seems massive as the silent minutes grow. It shows that neither of us knows how to approach the subject, so I continue. "Let's check it out." I switch on the lamp beside me and stride over to the mini-fridge. I must admit that I'm excited to see something I'm familiar with. No emotions. Just blood. I am certainly getting to the point of hunger, and if there isn't anything to eat soon, I'd have to eat my earlier words. Which means Ivy's vein for will be dinner.

Opening the mini fridge, I'm taken aback by the amount of blood bags stuffed inside, along with a decent number of mini bottles of vodka and a couple of candy bars. My eyes skip the Gray Goose, and grab the two bags of sustenance.

Holding them in both hands, I turn around, but before I can pass it over to her, Ivy has already taken hold of one bag. Two long fangs slash the tip of the bag and with both her eyes closed tightly, she glugs it down.

Once finished, she chucks out the empty bag into

the trash can. She looks over to me and holds out her hand soon after. "Are you finished?"

I quickly drink the red liquid gold and give her a nod, then hand it over to her. I would have been happy with a second bag to quench my thirst, but I'd prefer to ensure there is enough for both. More for Ivy, as she will likely be hungrier than me.

I shuffle over to the bed and Ivy appears beside me shortly, with a speed that I am proud of seeing her adapted to already. Once we both lay down, finally finding a comfortable position, Ivy says, "I don't know how long vampires sleep, but hell, I really am tired."

"Yeah, it varies with vampires as it depends on age. So, for me, not that much rest is required. I can last longer on little sleep and a lengthy period between meals if I have to. You, being newly transformed, can usually expect to be tired at times and require more rest. With the fierceness in you so quickly adjusting to your strength and thirst... well, I have a feeling that you're one of a kind."

Ivy chuckles. "Really? So, what about the saying, 'no rest for the wicked'?"

I can't help but chuckle back and shake my head, switching off the lamp, letting the dark envelope us once again. "Rest up, Ivy. Try to not hurt anymore trees tomorrow."

"Don't worry, Zachary, I'll be on my best behavior."

I close my eyes tightly, really wishing she didn't say that because my thoughts linger toward a very different mindset.

I wonder what Ivy is like when she misbehaves. Naughty behavior, to be specific. In bed, with her legs wrapped around me, to be even more specific.

Chapter Twenty-Two

IVY

I'm trying my hardest to fall asleep, but my thoughts are running wild as a frickin' stampede as I recount the earlier conversation.

Not only did Zachary enter into immortality all alone with next to no support, but it also seems that his immortality has also been rough with no tenderness and love. He also sounded like his past had turned him into a sad, lone wolf.

The fact that he asked me about my family and listened to me rattle on about dancing, band camp and Damien, even if it was only for a few minutes before I nipped the topic in the bud, it was sweet and… pleasant. Getting to know me with no talk of vampire business. It made me feel human again.

I still can't fathom how a vampire's skin can feel warm to the touch considering we ought to be cold, but despite that, the warmth that radiates from his body as he lies beside me is wonderful. I'm seeing similarities that defy all logic when it comes to vampires because everything about myself and Zachary, except for the fangs, thirst for blood, and dead heart, we sort of still function the same as before. Yes, the skin tone changes and most features, but that's aesthetic. I can still feel… cold and warm. Or feel lust, anguish, and sympathy. I thought vampires were simply dead monsters who would kill any human in their path to drink from them. Or maybe like Dracula. Regardless, this is definitely not what I expected to feel.

Speaking of feelings, when Stella messaged, my green bitch called jealousy reared its ugly head. Annoyingly, I immediately had to tamp my envy down. Zachary's not mine, I'm not his, and he clearly doesn't want to pursue anything more. In saying that, when he explained nothing was ever going to happen between him and Stella, I was beaming on the inside. No, I was secretly clapping my hands with a devilish smile, knowing she wouldn't have him the way I do. Or at least for now.

I play with the ends of my nightie, a flimsy thing I threw into my bag. The energy coursing through me because of my anxiety is irritating me, now impeding my sleep.

Shutting my eyes, I do my best to relax, but my brain seems to want to play a different game. An image of the blood bag appears, and am instantly brought back to the moment I saw it. Not going to lie, the bag looked delicious, but as soon as it hit my tongue; I had to resist spitting it out. It wasn't warm and smooth like Zachary's. It was just a stranger's blood. Knowing it was in a bag made me feel a bit better rather than finding some helpless human sitting down with her arms wide open, ready to be fed on. The imagery is revolting.

At least this way, I could just chug it down, discard the plastic into the recycling bin and do my best to forget what I drank and be happy I can sate my hunger.

Maybe I can make it better by pretending it's

Zachary's.

Now there's a thought to get me through the blood bag process. At least he wouldn't have to compel me to drink from him all the time. I really need to figure this out because I can't be under a compulsion to drink forever. I need to be independent, and if the Vampire King sees me weak, requiring magic to drink, it won't look good. Might not even end well for me, who knows.

I blow out a sigh and roll onto my side, only to realize that it's to my left, bringing me inches from a sleeping hot, lonely, and torn vampire. I just wish I could see him happy, or at least hear him talk of a good time in his life. He's sleeping at the moment; I can sense it. With this knowledge, I gently hover my fingers over his chest, especially his beautifully drawn tattoo, then over his arm and toned bicep, which my lips suddenly want to kiss.

Argh. Get yourself together, woman! He doesn't want you. Get the frickin' picture already!

Closing my eyes, I roll onto my back and rub my temples.

Shit, what's wrong with me?

My subconscious responds.

You are attracted to him. You can't deny it. There is nothing wrong with you. This just feels right.

Chapter Twenty-Three

ZACHARY

My eyes open automatically as the time on my cell hits 4.00 a.m. I rise from the bed, shower, and quickly change into my jeans and blue t-shirt I stuffed into my duffel bag on my way out of the estate. Finishing with my favorite black timberlands, I grab a blood bag to keep me sated for at least most of the day. I head out to the beach to check out the perimeter. I want to find out how many humans are around at this time. This way, we can determine if it's safe to do some practice on the beach.

A scatter of streetlamps along the pathway between the road and beach is all the light we are provided. I take note of how peaceful it is, and with luck, completely deserted. The scent of the salty air hits my nose and I breathe in the calming mist. Then, just as quickly, my body tenses when I realized it's dark now, but once sunrise hits, we won't be able to do much with people around. I hurry to wake Ivy.

I'm halfway walking toward the safe haven when I see her strolling toward me. When our eyes meet, her pace increases. Or is it my pace? I'm not sure, but it feels like a magnetic force. We slept so close last night, and if it were any other situation, I'll be honest, I would have propositioned her. I would have been honest with her and tell her how she fills my thoughts all the time. That I love her scent and everything about her. But that's in a world where there are no consequences. No Connor. No lies or deceit.

With unexpected enthusiasm, I smile and say, "Morning. I was just going to see you and let you know the beach is secluded and ready for us."

Ivy nods, quirking her eyebrows at me, almost as if she could sense my eagerness. All of a sudden, her expression changes and she shyly glances down at the sand, diverting her amber eyes away from me.

"The bed was cold without you. I was confused where you went to and, well, after being with you for even a couple of days now, I realized how lonely it is without you," she said, lowering her voice. Her expression is bashful, which is quite endearing.

It's a weird feeling, though, hearing her say those words. No one has ever said they were lonely without my presence. I force down my emotions and say, "I just went to check out the beach. It's all clear. Come on, we better do some cool-ass vampire moves before the humans come." I throw a smile at her, full of encouragement. At least that's my aim.

Ivy smiles and nods her head. She steps intimately close and I feel her breath against my ear as she whispers, "Run."

I smile as she attempts to pounce on me and quickly move out of her way, feeling cocky about my speed. Which turns out to be a crap move on my behalf because she expects it and does a low kick, just as I did to her yesterday. I'm yet again on my ass in the sand, by a move I showed her only once.

Shit, she is a fast learner!

"Don't get too cocky." I smirk, jumping up and speed toward her. It now turns into a chase as she zooms in front, laughing at the same time. I push myself faster, inches behind her when I reach out, grabbing her arm. Ivy swiftly turns and rips out of my grasp, jabbing me in the chest. Once again, she swipes her foot and trips me. That's when she pounces on me. Fangs shoot through and this is when I finally see the predator inside her rise. I'm pushed onto my back, with Ivy straddling me as we fight between anger and playfulness. "For someone who hasn't fought before, you're a quick learner." Her palm rests at my throat in an attempt to hold me down. It's amusing because her hands don't even wrap around my neck so it wouldn't work but, nevertheless, good thinking.

Ivy's fangs retreat, and with loud enthusiasm, she jumps up with a fist pump. "Woo hoo! Did you see that? I totally gave your ass a whipping!" Ivy stands above me, jumping in the air as I move to rest on my knees, rubbing the aching spot she punched at earlier.

Surely, she can't be this strong already.

I eye her as she continues yee-haaing and yay-ing. "Yes, I saw that. Doubt that'd be your reaction when you're in an actual fight." I smirk, trying to suppress a laugh.

"Aww, poor Zachy. Sad he got his ass kicked by a newbie?"

My eyes narrow. Clearly, she is loving this, and 'Zachy'? Did she just give an almost century-old vampire a nickname?

Full of frustration, I growl out, "First, it's Zachary, and second, you didn't kick my ass yet..." Just as her perfectly plucked eyebrows rise in confusion, I sweep my foot against her ankle. My favorite move. Only, I expected her to tumble backward, and in this case, she toppled over toward me. Landing right on top.

"Shit," Ivy grunts as she tries to hold herself against my chest, but the awkward position makes her hand slip, and she falls against my chest. "Oomph, sorry!"

I chuckle and offer a lopsided smile. "I won't lie. The view is pretty damn good from this position."

Ivy giggles, her body vibrating with laughter. I take in her flawless face, and then my eyes fall on her breasts, squashed against my chest. The feel of Ivy on top of me awakens my cock, and I have the urge to wrap my arms around her.

"Of course you are. You're a guy that knocks me off my feet and was lucky enough for me to land directly on top of you." She glances down at my crotch and says, "And gets excited about it too."

"Whoops?" I offer, to which Ivy smiles and gives another giggle. I find her laughs melodic, but she stops giggling when she realizes her breasts were actually rubbing against my chest.

There is a quiet moment between us, neither of us moving or separating from this position. My gaze catches Ivy's amber eyes darken whilst looking at me. I accidentally let out a grunt as my cock hardens more. I even notice the pebbling of her nipples through the lacey cups peeking from under her tank top. Our bodies are meeting, giving us plain evidence they want more than just banter. Before I have a chance to think, her lips press against mine, and I lose all my senses, forgetting the inner monologue about trying to avoid showing her any affection and distancing myself.

Nope. Instead, I deepen the kiss. She makes a little moan as our tongues connect, throwing all my logic out the window. Again.

Unfortunately, we both stop abruptly as we hear a rustling. In unison, we jump up, glancing around to see what's throwing our sense off kilter.

"Do you sense that? Is it just me or does something seem... off?" Ivy asks, stilling as she glances around the beach. She turns and yells, "Behind you!"

I don't get a chance to check as my face meets the sand. Not lightly either, but with force, to the point where sand is covering my eyes. Almost a century of being a vampire, my experience tells me the creature that has me pressed down into the sand is a mangy werewolf.

"You thought we wouldn't return to finish what we started? Bloodsucker, you should have finished us off when you had the chance. Now you get to watch her die, *Prince.*" The words surprise me as it's not often werewolves communicate in wolf form and speak English.

And then, its words rush back to me. I widen my eyes at the notion this mutt knows of my past. It's a secret that only Stella and Connor know about. Regardless of the revelation, I need to put that behind me and return to it another time. This is not the time for hesitation, especially as I hear a shriek I know belongs to Ivy.

I turn toward the sound and see her pushing off another large white wolf, which unfortunately is undeterred by her movement. It swiftly grabs her neck and lifts her, and a scared scream tears from her. Despite wanting to run and save her, I struggle to move under the wolf who is holding me down, only left to watch Ivy's toes dangle in the air.

Fuck, fuck, fuck! We are both distracted fools who are now struggling against an attack on us. What is going on with me? This would not have happened before I met Ivy.

With a husky tone, the wolf that has her in its grasp says, "We don't care who you share blood with. We have authority to get rid of you if you're a nuisance and in the way of what could ruin decades of peace."

Now, he might think I am on the same page as him, and I can say for sure that I'm not following. *Authority from who? How does he know me?*

I look over at Ivy, and our eyes meet. They are no longer red with lust, instead now back to amber with confusion, anger, and fear reflecting in her eyes. I can see the questions forming. I glance away, my focus at shoving off the mutt that has me pinned down. The less focus on her questioning eyes, the easier it is to disregard the truth that only I—and the wolves apparently—know. I won't give it away, at least not yet.

My thoughts suddenly snap into perspective, like a light bulb that has just switched on. The mutt mentioned getting in the way of ruining peace when referring to Ivy. Now it's slowly making sense. She could make or break the future of vampires. If she were to lead our Kingdom with a modern and better intention, then she very well could disrupt the long-standing treaty between the werewolves and vampires.

Suddenly, a foul breath meets my ear. "Whatever you're doing, stop it." I can detect the deviousness in his tone. "You won't save her. She is weak and so are you!" he growls.

Realizing that I'm not a fool to be reckoned with and taught by one of the better people in the vampire council to fight, I'm not the pussy this mutt assumes I am. I pretend to be defeated, sagging down further into the sand, making him seem victorious. But the mutt doesn't seem to know the moment a vampire shoots his fangs out, or how fast it happens. In a matter of milliseconds, I bite his leg like the unrelenting monster I can be. It's harsh and deep, making his howl piercing, but I don't let it distract me as I shove him off, twisting underneath to give me enough space to roll out from beneath.

Losing concentration, the wolf loosens his grasp and lets out a ferocious growl. With a force no human can ever achieve, I run toward Ivy, jump, and practically fly into the wolf holding her, my right shoulder successfully shoving it onto the ground. I may not be large in build, but I'm fucking fast and strong. And agility that can match his too. Ivy might make me weak, but that's a whole different and unexpected story.

Ivy crashes onto the sand with a grunt, but in a blink of an eye, she is upright and in a forward stance, ready to attack. I can see she is determined not to be wolf-handled again, black veins around her eyes, and her beautiful orbs now deep red. The wolves have awakened the monsters within us and won't like the outcome.

Both mutts quickly gather themselves and move closer to each other, two against two. Sunrise is on its way, but somehow it feels lagging as if it's waiting for this showdown to be over before it welcomes daylight. Ivy stands by me, her fangs now elongated to match mine. It feels like an inferno building the longer we stand facing the wolves. And then I make my move.

"You're deranged if you think you can kill me, and the future Queen. One day, you're going to need allies and so far, you're doing a poor job. You have two choices here. Run away and I'll pretend this never happened, again, and I won't report this to the Vampire King, or we'll sink our fangs into you and rip your throats out. Your choice."

One of the werewolf's growls and spits out, "You think we came here for an ultimatum? Bloodsucker, we came here to get rid of the vamp. We don't like the Vampire King, or any vamps in general, but trust me when I say we also don't like change. And with her being alive, that equals change, and we won't risk a supernatural fuck up because of her. So, if you think we are going to listen to you go on about an ultimatum, you're just as pathetic as she is." He then lunges toward me, with the second one aiming straight at Ivy, but seeing as she is prepared and quick on her feet, makes it all the easier for me. I don't have to worry about her and feel confident about her actions. I also need to focus on my own mutt.

The knowledge that I had already injured his leg bodes well in this case. With one speedy lunge back at the werewolf, I shove my shoulder into his chest, and it stumbles back, then falls to the sand.

With both hands, I grab hold of his broken leg, which drives the werewolf to howl in pain, completely losing control of the fight against me. I then thrust the animal a few feet away, just where the sand meets the shore.

I storm over to the mutt in the water, trying to

salvage whatever anger and pride he has left, knocking him back down. I quickly take hold of the injured leg. Snap. And the other one. Snap. Not before long, I stand above a werewolf in agonizing pain. The way it surprised us, and then attacked and threatened us, makes me want to do so much more than just break his legs. At that thought, my fangs elongate, and I kneel beside it and whisper, "Speak, wolf." I need to find out more on how he knows about me, or better, what else he knows about me. You'd think the mutt would be in enough pain to just listen to me, and give me a seed of information, but nope. He growls at me instead with what I suspect is a 'fuck you' and snaps his enormous jaws at me. *Fine, fine, I'll do it my way then.*

I walk around behind his head, grab hold of his neck with both my hands, and twist. Snap.

Just as the body stills and flops onto the sand, I remember Ivy was fighting her own werewolf.

I speed out to get closer to Ivy. However, I halt when I find her fighting in the sexiest way I've ever seen a female vampire attack. With a smirk and a 'Are you ready for me?' expression, she runs to the already bleeding and crippled werewolf and jumps high in the air. And I mean high like a ballerina flying through the air. The mutt has to look up, and as it cranes his neck to watch her, she gracefully lands behind him. The werewolf growls and turns around to snap at her, quite close in fact, but she moves aside in time to miss its jaws. She throws a low punch into its chest, just like we practiced, and the aim was great, knocking the mutt backward a little. As it stumbles, I can't help but cheer her on like a groupie.

Ivy quickly locks gazes with me and gives me a

cheeky grin. She then stalks over to the wolf, who is stumbling over and falls back into the water. I run over to her side and kneel beside the mutt. Ivy follows my lead on the other side and we both hold it down in place.

"Explain why we are targets and who sent you. Now!"

The werewolf struggles but gives in after a few shrugs and morphs into a frame of a man. His body is olive-toned, and a built physique, but that doesn't mean he can't feel pain. I don't hesitate in making him feel it.

I stomp on his leg, hearing a snap. He screams, and I can hear the excruciation in his voice.

"Now talk," I command.

The man struggles to move but eventually speaks. "Our leader. The Gray Clan. The old witch's vision was coming true. And…" He stops, catching his breath. "We were sent to hunt her down before she could make our lives worse. Including anyone that stands in our way. Regardless of the bloodline."

I can feel Ivy's stare, but avoid meeting her eyes.

"How? And how do you know about me?" The words are out before I can stop myself because, for a moment, I forgot that he could open a can of worms, and Ivy was right beside me.

"The Vampire King set a treaty between the wolves and vamps. If we were to supply him with humans, he would make sure no one touches us. The fact that we morph into human form makes it easier as we blend into their society. This is the arrangement we agreed to. This way, no vampire has a stake on us. We are free to roam and do as we want. We,"—he pauses to catch some air— "have a system in place and it works well for us, so we will do everything we can to avoid it changing." He attempts at shrugging us off, but I force him back down. He grunts and narrows his yellow eyes at me and says, "And we know all about the vampire that's accompanying her. How important he is because he is just as a threat to us as she is. Isn't that right, *Prince?"*

Fuck, too much information. In a moment of stress and frustration, I forget about getting more intel and... Snap.

The body stills, and Ivy gasps.

"Quick, it's now getting brighter outside, which doesn't bode well for us. Grab hold of his legs, and I'll take his arms." I motion toward his body.

"What? No!" Ivy throws a look of panic at me. "Water? I'll drown. I can't swim. Nu-uh, not happening."

Fuck, I forgot about that. I don't have time to debate this issue, so I bite the bullet and do it myself.

"Fine. Okay, just wait here," I say gruffly.

I lift the man and drag him into the water, walking fast yet carefully. Eventually, I swim out further, dragging him along with me until I feel that I am farther out than most people swim. I let go of him, giving him a strong shove into the water, not taking the time to watch him drown, then turn and swim back to the beach where Ivy is waiting for me.

"You just missed it! A massive wave came out of nowhere and just dragged the body out to sea for sure. "She pauses and then looks at me, taking in the soaking mess I am. She bites down on her bottom lip for a second and I can see appreciation in her eyes. I look down at myself and note the shirt I chucked on this morning, now stuck tightly to my chest and my jeans clinging to my legs. Everything was tight.

I wipe away the droplets of water dripping down my face. "Doesn't matter. It's normal for a body to sink first and then when the water fills their lungs, they eventually float up. So, unless some wizard-y shit happens and takes him to the bottom of the ocean to never reappear, I think we better get out of here and hope that nothing that happened this morning will come back biting our asses. But if it does, I'll ask Stella for some magical help. Which, in the paranormal world, means there is always something you can be indebted to. Nothing comes for free. There are no 'IOUs', and witches, well that's a whole other story altogether."

Ivy sighs and nods, but then furrows her eyebrow. And I know another question is forming.

"What happened to the other wolf?"

Oh right, I forgot to tell her what happens when a werewolf dies.

"I already took care of it. Unfortunately, unlike a vampire who perishes into dust, we need to consider disposing of bodies when it comes to werewolves."

"What do you mean turn into dust?" Ivy asks incredulously.

"When a vampire is killed, the body quickly decomposes and then,"—I snap my fingers— "they turn into dust. Werewolves, on the other hand, turn into their human form when they die. That's why I had to drag the body into the water. Now, let's go. People are already heading out to the beach. I don't want to ever return here after the fight we just had. Let's go, Ivy." Something about her makes me pause. "Are you all right? You're quiet, and I get antsy when people are too quiet." Especially her.

"It's just that I realize, a bit late though, that I... I helped kill. I injured somebody and then stood by, watching as you got rid of the dead body."

The way she exhales, deep in thought, makes me want to give her a reassuring embrace. I slow down my pace as I realize she is a few steps behind me, rubbing her gums. It was like an after-effect of actions that are far beyond what you would ever have done. The remaining human side is in shock. Ivy looks up at me and says, "My fangs... I used them for the first time in a fight. It's weird. Everything happened so quickly, I don't remember being thirsty, just angry. I wanted to kill the werewolf and my fangs shot out before I had a chance to react... Next thing I knew, they were deep in the werewolf's neck. Hell, Zachary, at one point I was sure I was going to rip out its jugular!" she cries out, waving her hands in the air.

I take a deep breath and exhale, knowing this must be giving her a roller coaster of emotions yet again. I needed to tread carefully. I walk closer until I'm standing in front of her and lightly squeeze her shoulder.

"Ivy, there is nothing you can do about it anymore. You protected yourself, and it also happened to be in the natural vampire way. Which you are now, so you must learn to understand, and live with the knowledge that this will be a part of your future. You will get angry, you will get thirsty, and that thirst will be to kill whoever stands in your way. In this case, the mutts were advancing on you, and you did the natural thing and retaliated with fangs."

I give her another light squeeze, which then turns

into my thumb, rubbing circles on her shoulder, just as I have done in the past. I feel her loosen up a little and all the anxiety and distress fleeing her body.

She glances at my hand, and I immediately stop. I open my mouth to say something and brush off my touchy-feely moment until she speaks instead.

"I understand and know what you mean. It's just a lot to swallow after being in action. Then sinking my fangs and tasting the blood… it wasn't, well…" Ivy stops and smiles as she looks at my neck. "I would have preferred tasting yours, though."

My body tenses, but it's from delight to hear that, and loving the pink tinge her cheeks now wear. I can't help but grin. "Not exactly what I expected to hear from you, but I agree with your sentiment."

Ivy giggles, and then suddenly lifts her arms around my shoulders and hugs me. It's weird at first because I can't recall a time when I was hugged. No one certainly ever showed me affection after a violent fight.

Like it's the most normal thing to do, I tighten the hug even though I probably should just pat her on the back and step away.

Ivy gives me a husky sigh as the moment between us gets warmer by the minute.

"I don't know what's happening here, Zachary, but I feel like I'm riding an emotional rollercoaster. Ever since my birthday, I have been so different. It's scary, even if I am a vampire now, it feels unnatural and…wrong." She pauses for a few seconds. "When I'm with you, that feeling goes away. Like when I'm with you, I'm content and…safe."

Taken aback by her admission, I find her comment

warming my dead heart because I certainly don't expect her to feel content with me. Sometimes I wonder why she isn't running in the other direction.

Because she is a strong one, that's why.

When the haze lifts, the word safe makes me feel terrible because Connor's face pops up in the back of my mind. It's like an annoying reminder that there is no future between us. Once she finds out who I am, whom I am leading her to, and how I lie to her every moment, her view of me will drastically change. So, I sigh and kiss her cheek, foregoing any romantic nonsense that I want to sprout to her.

"You did really well, Ivy. You should be proud of yourself and focus on that. Everything else will eventually become the norm for you. I hope you won't get caught up in too many fights over time, but with the way our supernatural world works, it's a never-ending world of drama. Besides, you kicked a werewolf's ass and avoided any injuries. That's pretty great for a newbie." *That's right, Zachary, play it light and subtly avoid her admission of feelings.*

Unfortunately, I notice her lips thin slightly, and my gut sends signals telling me that she didn't like my response or hoped for something deeper than what I sprouted.

Her back straightens, arms swiftly falling beside her, and all the warmth of her body leaves me. Clearing her throat, she says, "You're right. Thanks for the reminder." The air that surrounds me feels empty as she walks away, aiming straight for Stella's safe house.

Distance. I wanted it, and well, fuck, she pretty much gave me a wide berth.

Chapter Twenty-Four

IVY

The wind picks up as I walk away from Zachary, putting distance between us because my emotions are at a boiling point.

"Congrats, Zachary, way to blow a woman's ego," I mumble to myself.

My mind whirls with emotional thoughts, but the sound of a loud growl stops me in my path.

I look around, now closer to the park, which leads me to the studio. Yes, as annoying as it is to have to walk through a park from the beach to get away from Zachary, it's a good idea for the sake of giving each other some space from training. I swivel my head when I hear the growl again. Suddenly, the hair on my skin sticks up and I immediately hear alarm bells ringing in my head.

My curious self can't fight the intrigue and I follow the noise.

Quietly, I walk through the bushes, surrounded by leafy trees all around. There's a track up ahead that leads to a car park. The thought makes me frown though, as it only reminds me of going to the beach, picnics and throwing frisbees—all normal things I won't be doing anymore. Or really need to. I don't even know if vampires have fun like that.

I shake my head and continue until I see a black car.

My shackles raise when I see a large gray wolf pounce toward me, but out of shock, I'm fucking too slow for it and it smashes me against the car door.

The slam is hard, taking the breath out of me as the wolf is larger, stronger, and no doubt heavier.

Again, my defences are off! Now look at where I am.

"Get off me, you filthy dog!" I scream, baring my fangs as I try to shove the wolf away.

It stills at my words and lets me go, which makes me stumble in surprise. Not exactly what I was expecting. It snorts, then looks me right in the eyes, which seems so creepy. Yet, its eyes are absolutely mesmerizing. Like yellow glowing lights. And I am the deer stuck in the headlights.

Those eyes stay the same, holding me in place, but I don't miss the shape of it changing.

Right in front of me, its body downsizes, and, like magic, standing in front of me is a man. His hair is golden but messy and the gray t-shirt hugs his chest. The black jeans are tight and blend into the black timberlands cladding his feet. My eyes take in his body, but one thing that I don't recall focusing on is his…face.

My eyes rise quickly to his and, like a thunderclap, I realize who is standing in front of me.

"D-Damien?" I ask incredulously.

"I thought I was just a filthy dog," he responds.

"What are you doing here? Why did you slam me against the car like th—"

"I'll do it again if you don't shut your mouth," he

snaps, closing the gap between us.

I want to ask again because it's killing me not knowing what happened to the person who used to be my closest friend, but I listen and keep my mouth shut. It only seems to get me in a shitty situation.

Suddenly, his large hand grabs my wrist, pulls me, and opens the passenger door. In seconds, I am thrust inside the car and then the door slams, shaking the large car with its force.

Damien is inside the driver's seat just as quickly, and as I try to open the door to get out, he clicks the child safety lock button. I push down the button to open the window, hoping I could get it low enough and somehow climb out, but of course, he locks the windows.

"What do you want from me, Damien? Why won't you fucking explain to me why you've become some monster?" I roar, my fangs out and my eyes teary.

Emotional mess that I am.

He starts the ignition and begins to drive down a road that is definitely not leading me toward the studio I'm meant to be in right now.

The lack of response angers me further.

Fuck it.

I move forward and bare my fangs toward his neck, but the moment I get close to his shoulder, my face flies back. The force feels like a frickin' punch to the face.

I scream at the force of the pain throughout my face, feeling disorientated.

Damien just snorts and says, "Nice try, bloodsucker, but this car is designed to protect me from evil creatures like you. Especially you." Then he exhales and says, "Predictable, even if you are,"—he uses one hand to gesture bunny ears and says— "The future Queen." From the rearview mirror, I see him roll his eyes. "Doesn't matter, anyway, you'll never fulfill the Prophecy because you won't survive long enough to even meet the King."

"Screw you!" I yell, kicking and hitting the back of his seat because it seems to be the only thing I can do. "You'll see, I'll make things better. I'll do my best to rid monsters like you from this world," I snap.

Damien chuckles and shakes his head. "Wow, you're still stuck on saving the world? You clearly know nothing about your future. You believe in the good in this world, in this life, it makes you the epitome of naïve. You're ignorant, Ivy. But, as I said, it doesn't matter anymore."

I can't take this any longer and continue to kick and scream.

However, I stop when I smell the scent of water. It's not salt water though, nothing like the beach. More like earthy and musty. Sitting up straighter, I peer through the window and see the glimmer of a large lake.

"Why are we heading toward a lake?"

He makes a sly grin and says, "Well, Ivy, it works in my favor when I know the fears and weaknesses of my prey."

My jaw falls open at his words.

Water. I can't swim and he knows it!

"You wouldn't? No, Damien! No!" I scream and try to shove him away from the steering wheel, but only get knocked back by the protection spell.

Suddenly, the car feels as if it's going quicker than usual. Getting faster and faster as the speed increases.

"And a benefit to being a werewolf is that I can morph into one when needing to get out of sticky situations." And with that, he clicks a button near the steering wheel, opens the door, and jumps out, morphing into his werewolf form mid-air.

I scream.

The disbelief turns into outrage as I look straight through the windshield and see the path this car is going, heading straight toward a large lake. Large enough and deep enough. I know it. He wouldn't choose a shallow one—it wouldn't work in his favor. This is a well-thought-out plan by a predator.

Chapter Twenty-Five

ZACHARY

I'm taking my time to get back to the studio and face Ivy. Giving her some space to get there first is my best bet to let her simmer down a little. I was just trying to be cautious. Okay, maybe it came across as abrupt, but I tried to be as gentle as possible without falling into lust.

My footsteps falter as I sniff a scent carried off toward the highway.

I take in Ivy's natural floral scent and then, musky, wet dog.

"Fuck!" I clench my fists. "Ivy, where are you?"

My gums itch as I seethe with anger, my fangs wanting to rip the throat of the mutt that has Ivy.

I take a quick look around and apart from the lingering scent that my nose refuses to let go of, I only see a few cars drive past the highway.

I spin around and rush over to my car, buckle up, and drive it exactly to the spot where the essence is the strongest. The most pungent spot I can find and start from there.

With a quick swipe of the key card, I start the car and begin the chase.

****

The Tesla proves to have a great accelerator,

helping me get closer to Ivy as I follow their trail purely based on my nose.

Her natural perfume is delectable, floral and sweet, opposite to the stink of werewolf. A horrible mixture. Nevertheless, I use it as directions.

Finally, I see a car up ahead, reckless in its driving as it swerves between a couple of cars. The beeps and honks are blaring, but they don't deter the driver from slowing down or following road rules. I'm not far behind but press down on the accelerator harder because suddenly, the car swerves left onto a dirt road toward what looks like a forest full of bushes. It's surprising to see in Laguna Beach but I don't know the area well enough to pinpoint what's normal and what's not here.

"Fuck." This Tesla was not made for the bumpy ground below, rocking up and down. The car ahead is increasing its speed and mine, disapproving of the ground. All of a sudden, I see a wolf jump from the driver's side and disappear into the bushes.

My gaze focuses on the car, and that's when I notice the lake it's heading into.

No way! Come on car! Ivy can't swim. Go!

I press down on the accelerator as hard as I can, without a care about the car and how it handles the dirty ground beneath it.

Once close enough, I hit the brake hard, leaving the car to skid to a stop. I jump out just as the car Ivy is in flies into the lake. I run over to it but oddly it sinks quicker than I expected it to.

Don't they usually sink slower or bobble first?

Shit. I chuck off my heavy timberlands and run into the cold, murky water and dive in.

199

The water is dark and cloudy, but the car is large enough to spot. I swim closer to it and notice Ivy frantically banging on the window, desperate to get out.

I get close to the window, and she finally notices me and begins to hit it harder, fear cloaking the amber orbs.

Clearly, she isn't getting anywhere despite the banging. I grab the door handle, pulling, but to no avail. It doesn't budge.

I look at her worry settling in—the window isn't breaking, nor is the door opening. Ivy shakes her head and points at the driver's seat, but I see nothing. The car makes a bump and I realize it's hit the bottom.

I swim over to the windshield and hit it a few times with all my force, and finally, it breaks. With urgency, I swim inside, but Ivy isn't happy to see me. Instead, she shakes her head and points to the driver's seat, but I still don't understand what she is gesturing about. I push myself closer to her, but suddenly a force knocks me back.

It then hits me. Runes. The car is protected by runes. Ivy is trapped in the back with no way of getting out of the passenger seat.

I look around the car, and up above, directly above the steering wheel, are six runes. Quickly, I swipe them and chuck the runes outside, which then lifts the shield. Ivy seems to understand what I did and finally reaches out to me.

My hands clamp down around her arms into a tight monkey grip and pull her out. Wasting no time, I wrap my arm around her waist and swim up.

Once we reach above the water, Ivy is shrieking and clinging to me like a koala. It's ironic how someone who is a vampire is terrified of drowning. She's already dead, but then again, I do wonder if a vampire truly could die from drowning. There is only so much that we can withstand. Interesting concept, which I will speak to Stella about, but for now, I'll not mention anything to Ivy. I don't want to mislead her with assumptions.

"Y-you did it again, Damien tried…" Ivy stutters as she rubs her eyes. Droplets of water drop down her face, and the scent of the lake overpowering her delicious aroma makes me simmer because it's a reminder of the dark overtaking the light.

Her words are a statement, yet I sense she is seeking a response, but I don't have one for her. Instead, I choose to wrap an arm around her as we sit on the grass, trying to reassure her that everything is all right.

Her innocence and naivete are something I'm still trying to grasp—she is a bloodthirsty vampire, with super abilities and a future that will make her lead a vampire kingdom, yet here she is acting like a human. Emotional as she is snappy, teary, angry, and sweet. It's overwhelming. Sometimes, I think Ivy can simply pass as a human—there is barely a monster inside of her. Except when she drinks from me.

"Damien used runes to shield you from escaping the car," I say, dismissing her earlier statement. "He really is on a mission. Scumbag. When I get hold of him, I want to find out everything about his reasons for wanting to kill you, and then I'll rip him to shreds."

"Runes?" Ivy raises her eyebrows, skipping my heated comment about killing Damien.

I nod. "There is so much to learn about this world,

Ivy. I'm sure over time you will understand, but for now, let's just get back to the studio. You really worried me, and I just want to process everything that has just happened. My anger toward Damien is...well, I'd rather simmer down." As I finish, I remove my arm from her shoulders and push myself up from the ground.

Ivy remains quiet, nodding.

I have a feeling she is also processing Damien's attempt to kill her. She doesn't know but the true reason for wanting space isn't because of Damien. It's because I'm now realizing how much I care for her. Seeing her ripped away from me, hurt and terrified, just cemented the way I feel about Ivy. Although, I can't tell her as it will make it worse when she eventually leaves because she doesn't belong with me. I've got to remember that. She has turned into a vampire with the destiny to meet Connor and unite to lead the Kingdom. They'll likely fall in love, and I can't take that. I don't want to be around to see her happy with someone else, especially my brother.

Chapter Twenty-Six

IVY

We're back in the parking lot at the studio complex. I rest my head against the back of the car seat and do my best to relax. However, inside me, chaos exists.

Tonight, I realized two things. Damien truly is evil. A monster possesses my best friend. The other is that I believe Zachary is my savior. Something in the stars has aligned us, and I don't think it'll be easy to leave him. Although, I need to because I want to do something good and make a better world for vampires, to change things from the way they are now. Finding more innovative ways of surviving. Then again, this won't be doable if I stay with Zachary instead of meeting 'my destined to be'.

The whirlwind thoughts overwhelming me, and I wouldn't be surprised if there's an impending headache. I rub my temples and sigh.

Although Zachary saved me tonight, and I will be forever grateful. I wonder if the Vampire King would do the same. What if he won't care about me the way Zachary does?

"What's on your mind?" Zachary asks, breaking my conflicting thoughts.

"Just a bunch of thoughts swirling around in my

mind." I give a slight shrug and relay my thoughts on what level of kindness and care would I get from the Vampire King?

Zachary's response is unfortunately silence. Instead of talking, he hangs his head low and adorably furrows his eyebrows as if in deep thought. This all frustrates me because I want to know what he is thinking. Rather than simmering down over Damien, why doesn't he just want to stay with me and be close and gentle as he was at the beach? I miss his lips, even the blood.

A sigh breaks from me because I just need to voice my feelings. I'm driving myself nuts with mixed emotions and his mixed signals.

"I can't be with you, but I miss you even when you are with me. It's crazy and hurts my head just thinking about it."

Still, he doesn't say a word, but I know he heard it.

He truly is the master of keeping people at arm's length.

If that's the way he is, maybe I should just do the same. Compartmentalize my feelings for him and open that box when he is ready to fully hear how I feel about him. Even if it's for a little while.

With that thought, I open the door and step out, quietly shutting the door behind me. There isn't any reason to be in here when he wants to be alone. He'll come around eventually, but for now, I'm going to bed and do my best to wipe out any memories of Damien.

Chapter Twenty-Seven

ZACHARY

I close my eyes and rub them with the ends of my palm, frustrated at this internal conflict my brain is struggling with.

Why am I over-analyzing things?

My fist hits the steering wheel. "Shit." I want to roar from all the conflicting thoughts and emotions tormenting me.

Even worse, now, after tasting her blood, her lips, her neck, and touching the softness of her skin, I find it hard to fathom what it would be like without her.

I grab my cell phone from my jacket pocket and begin to dial Stella's number. I need to know why she didn't warn me of the werewolf attack and Damien. However, I don't get too far as suddenly a message pings up on my cell.

Unfortunately, it's from Connor.

"Shit, why now?" I ask, despite knowing no one is here to answer. I force myself to open the message, and it practically sounds just like him. Frickin' Connor.

—Brother, not that I care much about what you do with your time, I do, however, need your assistance with a particular issue that has arisen. In simpler terms, so you understand the importance of this message—I was left in a little situation with a woman that I was fucking. I got hungry, and she turned into dinner. I need you to clean the mess up. Find a way for this to not appear as an attack, as the last thing I need in Santa Monica is a parade of humans with pitchforks. Or for better terms, humans, and their social media. Don't take too long, will you? VK—

"Clean up your mess? Fuck you!" I quip, looking at my cell, wanting to crush it along with Connor's skull. I hate him so much. He is the worst of the worst and still dares to think so highly of himself. Then use me for help when he needs it. Hell, I feel bad for Ivy having to put up with him, eventually. It's no easy feat to do so.

How does the council put up with him, anyway? He's become a cocky dickhead as decades went by. Surely, they would want to kill him as much as I do. Not that I ever could, but the thought crosses my mind every time I think of him or see him.

My thoughts go back to Ivy and what she's doing. I don't have much time left with her before I hand her over to Connor. I rub the back of my neck, exhausted and annoyed at the turn of events. *Fuck, I'm behaving like an idiot. A beautiful and stunning sexy woman tells me she feels safe in my arms, tries to show affection toward me and I pretty much send her away. Such as idiot.*

I can't go inside yet, as I still don't know what else to say without misleading her again. So, I decide to just wait until she is ready for bed. It's daytime now, but I doubt that's the reason for her going to sleep. Ivy's had a tough day, or is it night? So much has happened in such little time, that time of day blurs into one.

I look back down at my cell phone for a second and

a sudden need strikes me. It's sudden but hard. I chuck my cell onto the seat beside me and take hold of the image of Ivy giving away all her thoughts and feelings to me like I am someone she loves. Willing to be open and trusting. The image of her face makes my decision final. I can hear the monster inside clapping his hands as if he's saying 'Congratulations, finally.' It's time I don't hide my feelings anymore. I'd have her for myself and take what I want. I have done nothing for decades, being a puppet to Connor, trying to steer away from the evil of the creature I am and never asked for much except acceptance. Not even penance, only for the last living—well, technically dead—member of my family to accept me. And do I get it? No, I don't.

And that's why right now, fuck everything. Here is a woman who has taken me on a crazy journey and wants me. Needs me. What if I never find that again? And even if I don't, this might not last between us, but I think we both deserve to fall into this lust. We may not have this chance again. Her more than me.

****

As soon as I enter, my eyes glance around the room, searching for Ivy. I get a slight feeling of excitement, which is odd as I rarely get excited anymore, but recently, my thoughts are constantly consumed by only her. Of her beauty, her innocence that's struggling to deal with the creature she has become. Her body that makes me drool, and the fact that she gives me hope. I don't know why the latter, but that feeling blooms every time I am with her. Perhaps that's the reason I have become protective of her.

"You know I can sense you standing there?" Her voice penetrates through me. I don't think I noticed how she sounded until this moment, oddly enough.

Realizing that whilst I was dealing with my thoughts, I forgot she was a vampire with the same skills as me.

My lips quirk, pleased to hear she's talking to me and not giving me the silent treatment.

"Did I wake you, or have you been lying there thinking of ways to tell me how you're fed up with me pushing you away?" I ask, knowing that I still need to apologize for dismissing her feelings when it was obvious. We both sense this connection blossoming between us. Sometimes, at rapid speed.

I walk over to the bed where she's resting, watching her stare at the ceiling.

That's not where her eyes should be looking.

I stride over to the nightstand, and the forceful movement works as her gaze snaps to mine. What I see is hurt in the depths of her amber eyes. However, quick as lightning, it turns to defiance, and she says, "Sort of...the latter." Her answer has a note of melancholy, and it pains me that I've been an idiot for constantly pulling her and pushing her away. Women get mentally exhausted and hurt by this behavior. It's a mind fuck.

I sigh and slowly shake my head, disappointed at how I handled things between us. "I assumed as much... Look, Ivy, I'm sorry," I say as I move to sit beside her, the soft mattress dipping slightly. "Truth be told, and I can't believe I am going to say this but, I'm fighting my urges toward you and for a variety of reasons. Some I don't want to go into. The key thing is that your destiny is to be with another vampire, and I am simply someone sent on a mission to unite you with him. I'm a puppet in this fucked up world we live in." I pause and shake my head. "But you're not. Nothing can come out of this, so I thought that the best thing to do earlier was to distance myself, even though I knew it would hurt you. Even after Damien took you... everything was getting so crazy. But, I don't know how much longer I can steer away from you."

I decide not to open up about my relationship with Connor. She'll be his, and it won't matter what happens after that. Ivy can fume at me later, but whilst she is with me, I want her to feel good and free from the foreseeable future she must deal with.

Ivy straightens up and leans against the headboard, pushing a hand through her onyx waves, frustration clear in her posture. She gazes up at me and says, "This is so messed up. I hate it how every time I try to show you how I feel and talk about my feelings, you hint that you feel the same and then it's like frickin' whiplash and you're back to Mr. Broody, detached from me. I'm not a fool, Zachary. I know that everything about this situation—me, you, and this Prophecy, is becoming a complete mess. Part of me wants nothing to do with it, but then if I have a chance to do something positive that would benefit me and the world I'm now part of, I feel that I need to see this out. A large part of me pulls back because there is a side of me that just wants to go back to my previous life." She takes a pause and turns her head toward the window, her eyes in a trance. "Back to dancing, singing, and to being free and not fretting over my future of being anything except myself. Carefree, and nice, unlike what I am now. I'm not nice anymore. I am an angry, bloodthirsty killer." Her gaze snaps back at me, and the amber eyes darken slightly as she continues. "And for some reason, you weigh me down when my feelings are conflicting. Like an unexpected anchor which I can't explain why I'm tied to. I said it before and I will say it again. Without you realizing it, you have saved me more than once already. You make me feel safe..." she finishes in a whisper.

Her eyes never leave mine as she opens up to me, gutting me in the process because I hate the fact she is going through this internal struggle. Yet at the same time, her words surprise me.

An anchor? I've never been an anchor to anyone before.

If anything, it's me who is looking for an anchor of my own. On instinct, my hand rises to cup her face, and I look into her mesmerizing amber eyes as if I'm searching her soul. Her words ignite a fire on my skin and then, without hesitance, I tightly pull her toward me and slam my lips over hers. Her breath catches for a moment, but she quickly opens up to me, her soft tongue meeting mine.

Ivy's slender arms wrap around my neck, her fingers gently roaming down my back, giving me a sensual feeling I've never encountered before. I move my kisses gradually down to her neck, rewarded with sweet, hushed whimpers that are for my ears only. They turn into moans as I suck at her neck, the spot where her pulse used to beat, driving both of us wild.

Swiftly, I lift her onto my lap and Ivy moves against me, rubbing against my crotch, and then delightfully rocks her hips. I squeeze my eyes shut to keep myself from moaning, as I continue kissing her neck, collarbone, and then back up to her lips.

My hands skim down from her petite shoulders, all the way past her waist, and then land on her luscious, tight ass.

I want to touch every part of her. The desire to taste her increases like a tempo that's reaching its climax. I imagine sinking my fangs into her neck whilst I move inside of her. The thought is like a promise from my subconscious, and this rhythm is getting faster and faster.

My head is in a fog of pleasure. There are no words between us, unlike the other times with women. Only our passionate embrace. I can't help myself as I hold her tighter against me and on instinct her rocking becomes a little harder, pressure pressing against my now all too tight jeans.

"So eager, like poison ivy spreading on someone's skin," I whisper as I lift my hands toward the thin straps of her nightgown, toying with them as I contemplate slipping them down her shoulders.

Ivy looks at me with a lustful gaze as her fingers slowly move toward the hem of my shirt. I grin and nod, enjoying this side of her. I let her finish and help remove it, not caring about the designer label getting crumpled on the floor.

Her eyes widen as she peruses my chest, touching every crevice of my muscles, seeming impressed with what she sees. I need a way to distract myself from her perusal, so I finally slip the straps down.

It takes delightful milliseconds for it to fall off her upper body, revealing two perfectly pert breasts. Her pink, hard nipples are greeting me again. This time, I need more touching, not just ogling. I lean down and take a suckle of each breast, and afterward, I grab her waist and tug her toward me.

My lips trace back to her collarbone and then I

catch hers again. I can feel a smile form against my mouth as she moves her hands down to the zipper that's trapping my aching cock. It's a prisoner in excruciating pain that can't wait to be freed.

I'm glad we didn't do this earlier, as the pent-up sexual tension led to us drowning in this heat and it's amazing. Everything we wanted is finally happening and fuck, I seriously want our clothes gone, and naked together.

Giving in to my thoughts, my hands grab her waist and swiftly lift her off me. Setting her on the bed, I stand to allow her to unzip the jeans.

I guess if she started, she may as well finish. If anything, I'm a gentleman and want to give her the pleasure of unwrapping me. Her anchor.

Ivy grins and leans closer. Her long waves fall over her shoulders like a curtain, and then with a lustful lick of her lips, I hear the sound of my zipper moving down.

Then she finally lets me free and eyes widen. She didn't expect me to be lacking underwear. But the shock disappears and the amber orbs turn lustful.

Her hand is inching toward it, excitement and arousal vivid in her expression. I can also smell her desire, a scent that is just as incredible as the feel of her palm wrapping around it. I watch her take hold of my hard length and slide her soft hand up and down, getting to know all the intimate parts. But the movement is driving me to insane heights, especially as I admire her two mounds moving up and down as she continues to drive me insane with her touch. She looks like an aroused vixen. But now, it's my turn.

Gently releasing her hand, I climb onto the mattress, moving like a predator inching toward its prey.

I cup Ivy's face, giving her a deep kiss. She moans, and the sound drives me wild. I grab her waist and lift her, playfully shoving her higher onto the mattress. She squeals as her body bounces, unable to suppress a giggle. It quietens down shortly as she gazes up at me, smiling like she finally succeeded in getting what she wanted for so long.

Balancing on one arm, I use my other hand to take hold of her petite wrists, my large arms easily wrapping around them. Much to my surprise and delight with no directive, Ivy lifts her hands above her head. I take that as an invitation, my vixen submitting to me. I gaze down at her gown that's still pooled around her waist. I take it by the hem and gently slip off the rest of the slinky material. The last piece of attire I find is the thin, black lace thong, covering what I believe is a luscious treasure.

Ivy gives me a shy smile, then bites down on her lip as I slowly drag the material down. It moves past her smooth legs and then I let it drop onto the floor.

And at last, there, laying in front of me, in all her naked glory, is the most beautiful and sexy female I have ever seen. I lean down and kiss her full lips, addicted to her delicious taste.

Realizing there is more to taste, I move my lips over to her belly button and give it a kiss. My mouth moves lower, peppering her with kisses as I move south until my head is between her luscious thighs.

Ivy makes the most delicious groan as I slide my tongue over her nub, hard and happy for me to take good care of it. Just as she spreads her legs wider for my tongue to appreciate what she has to offer; I leave and give some attention to those breasts that call for me. If I am going to have her tonight, I'm going to have every part of her.

I circle my tongue around the hard nipples in slow movements, gaining loud moans from Ivy, whose obedient hands are still over her head. I've never been one for complete dominance in bed, but her just giving me free rein and following through with the promise by keeping her hands in place delights me and turns me on too. I move onto the other nipple, giving it the same attention and once I feel they had enough, I return to her slick, wet treasure. Ivy screams as I delight her. I grab her hips and lift them closer to me, mouth ready for its feast. And to say that I ate her is an understatement. More like devoured.

My cock is throbbing so intensely by the time her moans and groans increase into a single, loud scream, leaving her body to a blissful shatter as the climax rips through her body. When she finishes riding the magical wave, I move up to her face to find her with hooded eyes, trying to catch herself from the wave of pure bliss.

The words fly out, and this time I have no shame.

"I can't think straight when you're around me, Ivy. Fuck. You taste amazing." And then I kiss her. Slowly yet surely. The complete opposite of the quick and hard thrust I make, leaving my cock tightly wrapped within her. She lets out a cry from the sudden entry, but then it turns into a mewl, and I love it.

A blissful smile appears as she opens her legs wider, her lithe dancer's body welcoming me in. Suddenly, Ivy stills for a second and blurts out, "Condoms?"

I am out of my mind with wanting to fuck the

vampire out of her and all I can muster out in answer is, "Infertile. No. Need."

"Goo-"

I don't give her a chance to finish as I slip my way out and then thrust back in, straight to the hilt. And I do it again, and again, thrusting into her like a crazed man. Even better, she meets me thrust for thrust, every motion in sync just like perfection. How can I be so deeply invested in someone I only recently met? I have no idea, but whatever it is, this feels amazing. It feels right.

Ivy kisses me, biting down on my lower lip, making my fangs ache with each nip she makes.

I quicken my pace and jut out my fangs, showing what I want to do next.

"B-bite. Me." Her words come out in stuttered moans, still pushing back as I continue thrusting.

Now, I slow the tempo. Balancing my weight on one knee, I grip her wrists above her head to hold her in place and sink my fangs into the delectable vein in her slender neck.

Ivy screams, and yet I don't pause because I know that it's from ecstasy, not pain. I can sense it in her, in her blood, pushing her over the cliff. As I drink from her, my hand leaves her wrist and ends up between her legs, where I pinch her nub. A little, yet powerful move, which sets her off. Ivy arches her body, crying out as her second orgasm hits.

I finally extract my fangs from her neck, licking my lips to catch any drops that escape, and take a look at her face, which only depicts pure euphoria.

What I don't expect, though, is for Ivy's hands to grasp my head, pulling me down closer to her and sink in her fangs into my neck. The move shocks me and equally arouses me even more than I am already. Ecstasy is all I can describe it as. Her sucking motion driving me insane, with soft lips moving against my neck, and hands grasping on to me.

All the sensations I feel build and build like an inferno rising uncontrollably. I let out a groan as I feel myself tense up and then explode. Into complete and utter bliss. Blood and all.

Chapter Twenty-Eight

ZACHARY

A ray of sun shines through the blinds, waking us up from our much-needed slumber. Not that we slept for long though, but for the few hours we did, at least we had some rest before needing to head off today.

Today!

The thought suddenly hits me straight into the chest, like a lightning bolt, awakening my giddy body to remind me that reality awaits. The reality that today I'll bring Ivy to the Santa Monica vampire den, where her future husband plays King. My mood sours at the thought, realizing that I probably won't have another night with her. Suddenly, I feel a warm hand on my shoulder.

"What makes you seem so down?" Her voice is quiet, almost a little croaky, which doesn't surprise me because she was screaming and crying out orgasms for most of the night—and morning. Now that was a good night. Well, that lifts my mood. I sit up and turn toward her, wanting to remember this scene after my life returns to black and white.

Ivy's hair cascades over her shoulders, amber eyes shining at me with… happiness? I can't explain it, but she looks less stressed and torn. Must be the endorphins radiating through her body.

Unfortunately, I burst this happy bubble by answering. "I was just thinking about what's going to happen when we meet with the Vampire King. When you finally enter the estate... Ivy, a lot will change." I didn't want to bring it up, but it was the truth.

Hah, truth. Not the full truth, just enough for her not to hate me right now.

Ivy completely skips the serious part and raises her eyebrow at me. "An estate? Like the one where you have vineyards or farms?"

I burst out a chuckle at her question. Naive but cute. Then again, she may not have been to an estate like Connor's, so I help her out a little.

"Not at all, unfortunately. First, vampires would have probably eaten the animals out of hunger and the vineyards wouldn't bring as much pleasure as it would for a human, if you get my drift." I grin and she laughs back at me, rolling her eyes at the sarcasm. "But in all seriousness, picture an LA mansion with lots of gates and security roaming the place."

Not that I will ever add the number of firearms with wooden bullets as protection stored behind every painting on the wall. The rooms where the humans are kept in, drunk from, and then 'played' with as they are compelled to enjoy whatever is done to them. Or the lucid details from all the famous parties the vampire council hosts, even since the 1920s when we were first introduced to this world. Nothing changed, except firearms became better and now used against paranormal creatures. Connor didn't change too much, although he lost more bolts over the decades, slowly declining into the mindset of a true monster. Twisted.

As I think the worst of what happens in the estate,

the sound of the door opening interrupts our conversation. I practically throw myself off the bed, Ivy following me, gathering up the crinkled quilt with her. I notice that it's covered with bloodstains. We washed each other during our shower so, it seems that whilst the blood from our passionate night was washed away, we must have forgotten about the bed and blanket.

Now that's going to be a stain that not even Napisan can fix.

"Don't fret, Zach, it's just me."

I recognize the voice immediately.

Fuck. It's Stella to ruin the moment again. Crap, what if she reveals the truth about me?

"Hey, uh, just give me a second," I say, hoping she'd at least give us time to change.

I glance at Ivy and see her holding the covers closer, skimming the room for clothes. Noticing her underwear and nightie on the floor near the bed, I quickly grab them and throw them over to her. She lifts her arms to catch them but doing that just lets the covers fall and leaves her gloriously naked. I give her an impish grin as she smiles, rolling those amber eyes that have come to entice me so much over the past few days. We find our clothes, and with stellar speed start putting our clothes on, despite them being crumpled, because… well, it was so worth it.

However, Stella steps inside despite us quickly putting our clothes on and pauses as we are almost fully clothed. Except, I was buttoning up the last shirt I stuffed into my duffel bag, and the cleanest so far.

Ivy, however, was great at getting dressed quickly, but rubbing through her sex/bed hair was a bit obvious. Or maybe we were just giving off so much tension and awkwardness with Stella's presence that it was easily detectable what transpired between Ivy and me.

I usually enjoy her company but wish Stella would at least give me some more naked time. But alas, Stella has to appear and pop it. My eyes flick toward Ivy, and I notice the frustration in her expression. Her blood sings to me and I sense the anger bubbling because of Stella. They are two very beautiful women, but very different at the same time. Ivy is…well, amazing. Sexy as hell and innocent at heart, but strong. Stella is cautious and caring, but the vibe I get from her is like a good friend, nothing more. Besides, I've seen her type in men and they tend to be very different from me.

I clear my throat and try to sound composed and casual; despite being honestly upset with her appearance.

"Hey, what's up? Is everything all right?" I rake my fingers through my hair and do my best to hide my annoyance with an awkward smile. I look at her and get the sense something is off. Focusing on her expression, I notice Stella's demeanor is different, very unlike her.

"They're onto you and with great intent on killing you," she says as she peruses the room and then whips her head toward me. "I expected you to get Ivy to safety, not to sleep with her. I foresaw a blur when I sought your presence, and now I know what the interruption was." Her eyes snap toward Ivy, and there's a slight change in her posture. Even more, I catch some purple in her pupils. Even the tone in her voice sounds vindictive.

Is she angry with me?

I rub the back of my neck and glance between Ivy and Stella, conflicted with knowing she is right in the sense all I was meant to do was deliver her to Connor. Then this uncontrollable urge to protect and possess Ivy kept on getting in the way. Before I begin to respond, I hear Ivy's voice.

"I don't think you are in the position of telling him what to do or what not to do. Frankly, that you just waltzed right in here unannounced, is rude. Even if it is your property."

The stern tone makes me inwardly smile. She doesn't seem intimidated by the three-hundred-year-old Seer. I mean, even I was at the beginning. Sometimes still am, truth be told.

"Zach, let's meet outside once you both get,"—she looks at us and waves her hand—"dressed."

Yep, looks like no matter how quickly we attempted to get dressed and try to act cool about it, she saw right through it.

Or maybe because I missed a button. Oh shit, I forgot to pull up my zipper.

My alarms are going off as I glance at myself in the mirror on the wall.

Ivy's eyes widen as she sees me turn and discreetly fix my zipper.

Fuck, this is awkward!

Stella sighs and says, "Look, I'm here only for a little while before I need to head to San Andreas for a reading." She speaks directly to me, ignoring Ivy altogether. Odd, though, seeing how important Ivy was for the paranormal world.

The tension is so palpable. I need to end this annoying and uncomfortable stalemate. I straighten my back and clear my throat. "We'll meet you outside in five minutes." Ivy is standing with folded arms, glowering at me. She can't see the invisible tug of war I am going through right now, how much I want to walk over to her, pull her amazing body toward me and smash my lips against hers. Then thank her for the comment she made earlier when she stood up to Stella. It was a first for me and I secretly wish it won't be the last as it makes her character sparkle and well, a bit of a turn-on. Some people think men need a weak or meek woman by their side but I've always been interested in feisty and strong women. Nothing wrong with sass.

But, I decide against my naughty imagination, knowing it would just increase Stella's interest and frustrate her more, even though I don't think it's any of her business in the first place.

I take a long look at Ivy and give her a 'please let's talk before you rip my head off' look. But all I get is a glare as she stalks toward the bathroom and shouts, "Make it ten minutes."

I have no doubt that was done on purpose, knowing it would annoy Stella.

****

Fifteen minutes later, longer than expected, we reconvene outside as planned. Ivy makes it clear she is borderline pissed, arms crossed against her chest, and glaring at Stella. The tension is loud and obvious, although I would have preferred the sexual tension we had earlier.

"Okay, so this is the plan—" Stella says but gets quickly interrupted.

"Plan? Are you seriously going to stand there and dictate everything we do?" Ivy exclaims with an incredulous look on her face.

Stella rolls her eyes and says, "Yes. I will." Then

she looks at me and continues, "Anyway, take my car, Zach, so when the wolves trail, they won't suspect you as they aren't looking for my car. Finding me in your car would derail them and slow them down. Of course, their scent is quite amazing, and they'll likely not falter for long. In the meantime, leave as soon as possible to get over to Santa Monica." Her expression is serious, and I know Stella doesn't seem impressed with the situation.

As I nod in agreement, Ivy gives me a look that could kill. I realize she is getting annoyed about Stella ruining our rendezvous, but regardless, Stella does have a point. And not to mention that she has helped us with providing the safe house. I can't just dismiss everything she has done for me. Turning toward Ivy, who is currently standing a few feet away, I muster a smile and say, "Ivy, she has a point. This is good. We have a getaway car at least. Why don't you get seated in and I'll be in with you in a few minutes?"

As Ivy walks over to Stella's silver BMW, it gives me a chance to speak and catch up with Stella.

I glance at her sense anger, even though, again, I don't see why I deserve it.

"You all right, Stell?" I ask warily, as this is a Stella I haven't met before.

"I can't believe you slept with her, Zachary! It's so…messed up," she blurts out, her eyebrows furrow in disapproval.

"Stella, don't start." I rub my hands through my hair again. It seems like all I do when I am around her, like a nervous tick. "It's not exactly like I expected to find her attractive or have my feelings all over the place. I know it's not particularly the ideal situation for us, but just leave it be. I...I know there is nothing that can come out of this." I pause and look toward Ivy, who is now sitting in the car. I shake my head and say, "So I get why you might be a bit confused by the way you found us earlier, but you don't need to be so disappointed in me. No offense, Stell, but it's not so much your business as it is mine. What happens between Ivy and me... even if it's for a night, stay between us."

Stella purses her lips and straightens her back, all defenses up. "Fine, suit yourself. Do what you want, it'll only backfire on you. I care about you and want to help you avoid stupid decisions, but hey, if you prefer to walk that line, who am I to butt in." She then turns around and stalks over to my car, only to stop and look at me. I don't understand why until she quirks up an eyebrow at me and holds up her hand.

Oh, right.

A deep sigh leaves me as I grab my key card out of my pocket and throw it at her. She catches it easily, then opens the door, her demeanor all business-like. Just before she bends down to get inside, I blurt out, "Stella, for what it's worth, thank you for everything. I'll see you when... well, when this is all over."

"No doubt we will." She shuts the door and turns on the ignition. Sooner than I had hoped for, my poor Tesla is on its way to fuck who knows where in San Andreas.

For some reason though, I have a feeling Stella will be soon saying, 'I told you so.'

"Zachary, are you coming or not?" I hear Ivy shout from the car as I watch Stella drive off.

I turn my head and nod, then stride over to the car,

both eager to be beside Ivy and also slightly nervous about the discussion we'll no doubt soon have.

Once I'm all buckled up and adjust the mirror settings, I take a moment to cool my nerves and look at Ivy. She's sitting next to me with her sexy lips in a pout, her seat belt on and arms crossed against her chest, which just increases the view of her delicious breasts, reminding me of last night.

Switching on the ignition, I back out of the car park, then stop to start the GPS directions toward Connor's estate.

Once on the road, Ivy still sits there festering in her emotions after this morning. Although I'm torn by what happened this morning, I decide it's time I explain myself.

"Look, Ivy, I'm sorry for earlier. I just don't want to pique Stella's curiosity. What happened between us was not part of her vision and Stella doesn't enjoy being blindsided."

Ivy nods, thankfully understanding where I'm coming from, but then she becomes quiet for a while. I glance at her and notice her biting down on her lower lip, and staring straight ahead, as if lost in her thoughts. Then she softly blurts out, "Do you regret it?"

My eyebrows arch in surprise, taken aback by her question. At first, I reel in an eye-roll at the cliché question and then contemplate on what version I should tell her. I choose the honest one.

"No, I don't regret it," I say slowly, making sure she understands the truth to my words, "but I wish it happened under other certain circumstances."

I sense her gaze as I watch the road ahead. "Do you mean the fact that I am supposed to be this grand

Vampire Queen?"

My lips curve, failing at suppressing a grin at her sarcasm, but alas, it is fitting. "Well, that you are the prophesied Queen poses an issue, but let's not forget that you are new to this world. Being propelled into a powerful position without experiencing life as a vampire first. Your mind and spirit still scream 'I'm human', when your body says, 'I'm not'... does that make sense?"

I grip the steering wheel tighter, wishing I could add that she is my future sister-in-law and 'FYI, your fiancé is a dickhead, oh, and 'I also have strong yet complicated feelings for you', but I hold my tongue.

"Why is it 'Queen'? I mean, I didn't think there would be actual royalty in Santa Monica, especially since Kings and Queens reign predominantly in Europe. It's just confusing...how can someone dictate what I will be?" The exasperation in her voice is loud and clear. So many questions and the irritation of knowing so little.

"Well, the original vampires were actually from England, but after a century, there was a war between rogues and the Royals. The Vampire Council was on the side of the Royals and helped fight, but they surprised everyone when a mutiny inside the court happened, and a large amount went rogue too. Eventually, there were more rogues than royals as well as the devoted Vampire Council. They decided to run, even though it was beneath them. They wanted the line to continue, so they chose to split into groups and go to different continents. From there, they did whatever they could to continue their lines. The King had to split from the Queen. Princes and Princesses separated too. Even parts of the Council had to split." I shake my head in disappointment. "Even though I wasn't around for it, it's still a shame that family had to be separated and forced to pro-create so the blue line would flourish."

"Wow... So who came to California and set up camp here?"

I chuckle at her question, amused by how she phrased it. "Well, no royalty came to LA, but a few vampires that were part of the council found out about a prophecy of a King and Queen being born in California and decided to set up camp, as you say here. They grew in numbers and prepared for what was coming."

"Wait, so the King is like me? He was also a human?"

Fuck, I shouldn't have said that. Now she'll think he is like her, but he's anything but like Ivy. Not a caring or sweet bone in his body.

"Ah, yeah. Just like you. But, Ivy, not all vampires hold on to their humanity. Just want you to understand that."

There, I gave her a warning. Hopefully, she will get the picture I'm painting.

She nods, furrowing her eyebrows, and then turns her head toward the window. Her gaze lost on the blur of cars and scenery passing by us. "What if I hate it? Do you think the King, or the council, will let me walk away?"

I sigh and give her the answer I have been formulating in my mind from the moment my heart warmed for her. My body was taken over by our sizzling chemistry.

"I've been wondering the same thing, to be honest. The witch who saw this vision also envisioned you bringing goodness to our kingdom and making our lives for the better, not for the worse, or stagnant as it is now. Who knows what will happen when you meet the King, but the chance is there and I guess no one knows until it happens." I hate those bitter words because it's a lie and then there is the part about how much I don't want her to meet him.

Balancing the task of watching the road and checking on her, I take the risky glance at her and notice that she's biting her cheek. Her expression screams disappointment.

It is obvious that the wheels in her head were turning, and my curiosity peaks.

"What's going on inside that beautiful head of yours?" I ask, wanting to know what thoughts she is keeping to herself.

Ivy gives me an incredulous laugh and gesticulates her thoughts.

"That this situation is complicated. That I'm hungry and crave your taste. How I feel there is no way out of this Prophecy. That I have no idea what I'm doing and really dread it. Or how I want you to stop driving to Santa Monica and just…"

"Run off together into the sunset?" I finish for her with a smirk, which grants me a laugh.

"Somewhat," she replies quietly as she sobers from the laughter.

"I know," I whisper, and despite my mind spinning with all the rights and wrongs on this whirlwind instacrap that's happening between us, my hand finds its way to hers. I give her delicate hand a light squeeze, which makes my lips curve into a smile. I like the warmth of her touch. I just wish Connor would have an expiry date. I wish that Stella wouldn't have to make me rethink my choice and make me feel terrible about sleeping with Ivy. The thoughts only worsen my mood and leaves us in silence as we drive toward our impending doom.

Chapter Twenty-Nine

ZACHARY

The day began sunny and warm, even the sunshine shone through the windows, capturing Ivy's beauty. I try not to sigh or smile whenever I glance at her. But now, like a bitter irony, the day has become chilly, almost symbolic of the cold and bleakness that lurks in Ivy's future.

I park the car a block away instead of the driveway that leads to those steps that I so clearly remember walking up when I first set sights on this house. Why did I park so far away? Because I still want distance from my life and want Ivy close to me despite her future inside the house of horrors.

"So, this is it..." Ivy murmurs. I could hear the uncertainty in her voice and a selfish part of me feels pleased.

Suddenly, and unexpectedly, I do what I told myself I wouldn't do. I give her an out of all this madness.

"You could run, you know?" My words are slow and cautious. It even tastes odd as the words roll off my tongue. Ivy's eyebrows shoot up, matching my own as I process my own words. Running would be a bad idea...but the concept tumbles out of my mouth.

Am I really doing this? Giving up a way for my

freedom... to get away from Connor for good?

Glancing away, my gaze ends up at my hands wrapped around the steering wheel. Simmering on the reasoning behind my silly comment. I finally revert my eyes to her.

What I see pleases me.

My brain and groin are both excited by Ivy's reaction. Her body leans toward mine and a hopeful smile settles on her face. I even think I saw a twinkle in her amber eyes.

"Wait, you're considering it?" I ask, not knowing whether it was to myself or her, but nonetheless, I ask the question.

Ivy shifts in the seat. "I was never one to give in when in a fight or confronting situations. To be smart and logical. I'm torn between seeing this through because there is the potential to make things better. Then again, I feel a magnetic connection to you, even though I barely know you, and sad to have you away from me. I will miss you."

"Well, technically, you do know me well. Maybe not the vampire version, but you know more than I've ever exposed about myself—my past, my thoughts. It's not a usual thing of mine to talk to someone and tell them my story."

Ivy smiles and places her hand on mine. "That's fair enough. You opened up to me, so I guess I do know more about you than I ought to. You were only meant to be the messenger and guide." Ivy makes a pregnant pause to then suddenly burst out with a giggle. "Oh, Zachary, if you weren't a vampire, you could be like a guardian angel!"

I roll my eyes and chuckle. "I can't believe you just

compared me to a guardian angel. They are good, bring the best out of people. Sweetheart, I'm the one that delivers you to hell on earth."

Soon after my words, her smile fades and suddenly I feel guilt build up in my chest.

"Do you feel like you're at a crossroads? As if you are in a game of tug of war."

I blow out a exhale as I process her question. How can I possibly tell her that I've been in a game of fucking tug of war since I first laid eyes on her? I tried avoiding the question earlier by sarcasm and changing the topic... but now? I am tired of hiding.

"Ivy, I—"

"No, actually, don't answer. Forget about it, it was a silly question anyway," Ivy hurriedly says as she sits up straighter and twirls her hair. Awkward silence fills this car yet again. Her strawberry scent also filling up the car, reminding me of her delicious lips.

I gently grab her chin and turn her face toward mine. The startled look in her eyes dims down as she quickly glances at my lips. Her gaze then works its way up my face until it meets my eyes.

"Ivy, I *am* at a crossroads here because I know you want to go and meet the Vampire King. But I also would love to turn this car around and whisk you away. To keep you all to myself." I move my hand toward her hair, slipping my fingers between the loose tendrils that have come out from its restraint. "You have to understand that it's unusual for me to feel...this way about someone. I don't generally dislike people, but I am not the warmest creature and my attraction toward someone has never been so strong. But enough is enough. I can't deny it anymore. I am tired of the puppet strings my dead heart is strung by." I pause as Ivy's mouth opens and closes, clearly surprised at my declaration. "So, to answer your question before you tried to dismiss me earlier is that yes, I do feel the same way you do."

And then I cup her face and slam my mouth against hers.

Ivy deepens the kiss quickly too, as if she couldn't wait for our lips to collide. It feels like I'm floating on cloud nine. Her hands slip around my neck as she pushes herself against me in a delightful haze of lust, despite the uncomfortable feeling of leaning over the shift stick.

But my mind is swirling with the notion she still doesn't know the whole truth. That I ought to tell her how I made the part of the Prophecy up just for her to follow my lead. For selfish reasons, I planned on giving her up on a silver platter to an evil vampire who will probably kill her after he gets bored with her, Prophecy or not.

The thought makes me stop, and I gently release our lips from the heavenly kiss. I wish we could continue, but she needs to know whether she chooses to run with me or go to Connor. Now's the time, for better or for worse.

I let out a loud exhale and look her in the eyes.

"There's something you need to know too... I wasn't telling you the entire truth. I should've told you earl—"

A movement against the door breaks my moment of truth. Ivy quickly turns her head, following my gaze at the figure leaning against her side of the car.

"Do go on, I didn't mean to interrupt this moment.

Go on, Zachary, you were saying?" the voice oozing with sarcasm and arrogance.

My gaze narrows and I feel the anger stirring inside.

How the fuck did he find us?

"Connor, what are you doing here?" I ask slowly, enunciating each word so he could hear the anger he invokes in me.

I want to smack that smug smile off his face, the masochistic gleam in his eyes. He truly is a nutter. A nutter that wants to rip Ivy away from me.

At the thought of that, I look at her and see confusion written over her expression as she looks at Connor—who is switching his gaze between us both. Ivy glances at me for a moment and then swings her head toward Connor and then back at me, and I swear I see the flicker of understanding that there is more to my story than I let on.

Chapter Thirty

IVY

Brother? Am I hearing this right? My gaze leaves Zachary's and falls onto the immaculately dressed man leaning against my door. His expression boasts superiority and confidence.

How did Zachary have a brother all this time, and never tell me! Twins, for goodness sakes, that's not the end of the world. Is he worried that I would prefer him instead? Like sibling jealousy?

I turn to him, shocked at the secrecy. "Zachary, I don't understand… why didn't you tell me you had a twin brother? How could you withhold that information?" I try to keep my tone calm and reel in annoyance at him for keeping this from me.

His brooding eyes, the emerald jewels that held me captivated since the moment I saw him, catch my gaze and I can see he is fighting his angry emotion. His expression is stark as he says, "It's not just that, Ivy. We don't have the"—Zachary looks over at Connor as he continues— "best relationship, as you would think. It's complicated. I'm sorry I didn't tell you, but it's not so simple…" He trails off before he snaps his gaze at Connor.

"What? Come on, Zachary. After everything we've done, surely you could just explain it to me," I say as I gently put my hand over his. "Would you prefer to talk to me privately? Is there an unpleasant history between you two?"

Before Zachary could answer, his brother intrudes on our little discussion with a knock on the car.

"Still here by the way and as cute as you are trying to find out more about me, I'll save you the trouble. I'm the long-lost brother."

There is no finishing to that sentence as in a flash, Zachary is out of the car and suddenly in front of his brother.

"How did you find us, Connor?" Zachary bites out. I can hear his shock mixed with fury at this sudden appearance.

Wait—Connor? So that's the name of the identical hotness outside my door.

"Okay, this is getting silly," I exasperate as I unbuckle my seatbelt and begin to open my door.

"No, Ivy. Don't get out. I think you should just stay put for now," Zachary says quickly, giving me a worried look, his hand gently pushing the door back toward me. I can see he's trying to protect me, but I don't understand why.

"I disagree, actually," Connor says, giving me a grin and opens the door anyway, gesturing for me to get out. Intrigued by this development, I agree and step out of the car. I have this crazy need to flex my toes and stretch after being in the expensive contraption that Stella lent to Zachary. But this is a little dramatic and there is so much awkwardness, it's bordering uncomfortable territory.

Zachary tries to move toward me, but Connor is swift and puts his body a few inches in front of me.

Like a protective stance, but by the look in Zachary's eyes, if anything, it looks like he is the one that's worried.

"Connor!" Zachary blurts out, but the moment it comes out, I see the shock and fear in his eyes. As if that's not something he ever says.

"I'm your King, Zachary! That is the only way you introduce me," he says, giving him an evil glare, throwing daggers at Zachary just by a simple look.

King? My eyes widen into fucking golf balls as the word simmers around in my brain. If Zachary is a vampire, his twin would be a vampire too? But King?

"Zachary... is your brother the Vampire King?" The incredulity in my tone is loud, but once the words are thrown out, I have a feeling I won't like his answer. "What in world is going on here?"

Connor opens his mouth again, unwanted input because this really feels like a rollercoaster ride of emotions that I need to sort out with the man I am falling for.

"Questions, questions, questions," he says, tapping his lips. "Understandable, of course. It's a shame that you have been put into the middle of an awkward situation."

"Zachary, answer me. Look into my eyes and tell me the truth. No looking for loopholes. No riddles."

His eyes find mine, and I hate the way his gaze holds me because it makes me want him so badly. With pursed lips, he nods his head in defeat. I notice he begins rubbing the back of his neck, the frustrating habit that I have come to know so well.

"Yes, Connor is my twin brother, as you can see. He is also the Vampire King. The same one in the

Prophecy that is tied to you... he is the one I guided you to. My aim was to just help you learn a little more and with the deduction of the attack, it was just supposed to be a simple guidance." He pauses for a second. His expression is pained, but it's his answer that makes me forget his pain. I'm the one in pain. Zachary takes a cautionary step toward me and lowers his tone. "But the moment I saw you, I struggled to think straight. Ivy, I have been struggling, fighting my obsession of wanting to be with you, hold you and...and at the same time, knowing that you are going to be with my brother. I know it looks bad, but I had the intention of telling you in the car. I was going to fess up everything before we would take the step..."

The confession feels as if a bucket of ice is poured over my head. Each word an ice cube plonking atop my head. I want to say something, but it feels like my mouth is wired shut.

A hand covers my shoulder, which makes me tense up.

"My dear, I'm so sorry that you have been betrayed. He lied to me too, you know. I never knew that I had a twin either..." Connor says as he draws a sensual line up and down my arm with his index finger.

"Take your hands off her! She isn't a piece of meat. And you're lying! I never knew—"

He is just about to finish his rebuttal, but Connor beats him to it.

"Well, aren't you a bit of a hypocrite!" he quips back in frustration. "Aren't you the one that took her at her most weak and vulnerable time, fucked her, and then spat her out in the end because she was never meant for you? That sounds like treating a woman like a piece of meat to me. Don't you think?"

I watch as Zachary opens his mouth in surprise.

"How...how did you know?"

Connor chuckles like we're all having a fun conversation. "Ah, yes, well, I was not aware until now. You just confirmed it." he finishes, his eyes morphing into a deep red haze as he licks his lips.

Listening to them just makes me feel more anguish. It feels like a kick in the guts.

The emotions swirling inside of me are like hot lava, bubbling underneath the volcano. I just want to scream to free myself from the ongoing torture of mixed feelings. Especially as Zachary has the audacity to just stand there, and I know that Connor's comment hit home.

I see Zachary's shoulders sag and just like that, I see defeat. Not even one rebut to save face.

The rational part of me knows he didn't treat me like a piece of meat, but the furious side of me still grabs onto the fact that he made me trust him. Fed me sweet words, had sex with me, and outright used me. I can't just give him the benefit of doubt.

No. Damien hurt me because of my future, and so did Zachary. I won't let it happen again.

"Enough!" I shout. The lava is pouring and I'm going to erupt very soon. I peel my arm away from Connor, who still has his hold on me, and stomp over toward Zachary.

The neurons in my brain are livid and I act on my anger. With a force I've never used before, my raging hot hand surprises all three of us when it meets Zachary's face.

He stumbles back, with a palm against his cheek.

To a human, they wouldn't see the flicker of confusion and anger in his eyes. But with my eyesight, I see everything, crystal clear.

I look over my shoulders toward Connor whose mouth is a little ajar, surprised at my action too. It flickers away all too soon and is replaced with a grin. It's smug, I know, but the hint of pride is there, and it makes me stand a little taller.

I spin around and walk toward him, turning away from the vampire that captivated my heart and broke it just as quickly. Connor's grin widens as he reaches out his hand and says, "Come, dear, there is a lot to discuss."

Slipping my hand into his, I let him walk me over to his car, which is yet another extravagant contraption except this time, according to the logo, it's a fancy white Porsche.

He opens the door for me, and I get inside, the atmosphere cold and dark. It's a car, it shouldn't feel like anything. But I quickly realize that it's coming from me. I feel the gloom.

As Connor walks over to his side and slips in, I take an unhealthy glance at Zachary, standing there with his shoulders sagging, hands in his pockets, and a heart-breaking frown. His eyes are pleading, but I remind myself that he used me and lied to me at every turn. Every chance he had to be honest with me. I'm not entirely sure if I would have stayed with him, or returned his sentiments, but I at least deserve the truth. He says he wants to hold on to his humanity. Well, the humane thing to do would just be honest.

I turn my head away and look at the identical vampire sitting beside me. Yet even though he is taking me away from a liar, by the cocky expression he wears, I wonder if deceit runs in the family, too.

Frustration grows inside, and I rub my hands up and down my legs. Connor's voice surprises me out of my stupor as he says, "Don't you worry, my Queen, you'll forget about him soon. Our future awaits, so you should focus on that instead."

Clearly, he does not know that I was falling for Zachary and that it won't be as easy as he may think to just forget him. But that's for me to know and for him to never find out.

I nod and do my best to not watch how Zachary's figure is getting smaller and smaller in the side-view mirror. But I fail miserably. Falling back into the seat, I slump a little, feeling slightly defeated.

Trying to keep my mind active over something else that isn't my non-existent relationship with Zachary, I turn my head again to look at Connor and see if I feel anything for him.

Is there meant to be a spark between us? Like with Zachary?

My mind is in jumbles, and I hate not understanding what is meant to happen between me and the King. How will I become Queen? There are so many unanswered questions, and I honestly, really hope that someone will have answers soon.

"You know, I've been thinking," Connor starts talking to me as I struggle to sort out my thoughts. "What is your goal in all of this?"

"Umm, I don't know what you mean," I say, now all too curious to hear his explanation.

"Like, in a book. What is your goal in the plot?"

My eyebrows lift in surprise. What a strange

question.

"To fulfill the Prophecy and hope to make a better future for vampires. Like what the witch saw in her vision," I say proudly. If I can't be a dancer anymore, then at least I do something good, even if it's for a world of monsters. Something good needs to come from me. I don't know what else I would do if I would just sit back and watch evil succeed. Satisfied with my answer, I wait for his reaction.

Connor looks at me in awe, his emerald eyes wide in shock. And then he bursts out in laughter, echoing inside the car.

I cross my arms, annoyed with the way he's carrying out. He's laughing at me and it's plain frickin' rude!

"Excuse me, what's so funny?" I snap at him.

He chuckles and shakes his head. His eyes focus on the road and just as we pull into the driveway, he turns and looks at me.

"My brother seems to be quite the liar."

I frown at his words, trying to understand what he is implying, as my stomach is tied in knots.

"Ivy, your goal is a terrible fuck up," he says with a smile, "and why, you may ask? Well, because a better future for vampires isn't part of the Prophecy. They will unite as one and follow together, which is the truthful part of Zachary's story. However, the Queen will rule with her King on the side he chooses. In other terms, I like to feed on humans. I like the status quo. I like the way I rule. This will mean that you will follow in my footsteps. So, sweetheart, there is no saving anyone, not even yourself."

"What do you mean? No, Zachary told me—"

"Of course he would tell you anything to get you hooked. And you, my dear—hook, line and sinker. Although he may have had his reasons for deceit, he did reek of tragic emotions. To think he could start to fall for you after twisting the truth to benefit himself is funny. Foolish nonetheless."

Did Zachary really lie that much to me? Had he twisted so much of the truth, and then added more bullshit just to use me?

Yes, he fucking did!

I'm livid with all this information. It's too much to grasp all at once. One thing I know is that at the beginning of this drama, I cried tears of betrayal toward Damien. Now, it feels like déjà vu. I'm back at 360 degrees to wearing the same emotions of betrayal, just from Zachary instead.

And now, with no way of doing anything positive with me being Queen, I feel empty. Damien and Zachary have ruined me. They have emotionally ripped me to shreds.

All my thoughts come down to one question.

What the hell have I gotten myself into?

A word about the author…

Growing up with a passion for writing, Tania Gold, a wife and mother of two from Sydney, Australia, has always enjoyed delivering exciting stories to an audience. An avid reader of Fantasy and Romance novels, she had dreamed of creating her own world full of exciting and loveable characters.

Thank you for purchasing
this publication of The Wild Rose Press, Inc.

For questions or more information
contact us at
info@thewildrosepress.com.

The Wild Rose Press, Inc.
www.thewildrosepress.com